Illusional Reality

Also by the author

Illusional Reality Duology

Illusional Reality

The Quest

YA supernatural thriller

Stone Cold

Collections

Heads & Tales

Undressed

A Flash of Horror

Illusional Reality

Karina Kantas

Illusional
Reality

SECOND EDITION
Published by Asteri Press 2020
Editorial: Michelle Dunbar, Annaproofing, Cayleigh Stickler, Rachel Shipp Editing

ISBN-13: 978-1-912996-13-1

Karina Kantas: https://https://urbanhype101.wordpress.com/

For Laura

CONTENTS

Mistaken Identity

BECKY PULLED HER COAT TIGHT TO HER chest. If her bashed-up Mini Cooper had started for work that morning, she wouldn't be walking to the taxi rank now. She walked briskly through the dimly lit streets, turning her head now and again to make sure she wasn't being followed. The neighbourhood just wasn't safe anymore. Luckily, there were only four people waiting: a teenage couple who had no problem with PDA and two elderly women nattering as their loaded shopping trolleys sat beside them. There were no taxis waiting outside but it didn't take long for two to pull up right behind each other. Within ten minutes, she was next in line for a cab. The manager bellowed a number, and a sour-faced man stood up from the back room. Becky watched him glare at her as he slammed his half-drunk cup of coffee on a table and then walked through and gestured for her to follow to his cab.

"Where to?" He moaned as he started the engine, switched on the Taxi light and set the metre.

After giving her address, she sat quietly in the back and listened to him cursing every motorist he passed. It was eight o'clock already, and usually took an hour to get home. Maybe less at the speed he's driving.

Becky lived on her own in a newly converted loft. She loved her independence, and being her own boss meant she didn't need to think about anyone else. She cooked when she wanted and ate what she liked, and she was determined to keep it that way, which was why she turned down her colleague Frank. He was forever asking her out and refused to take no for an answer. There was nothing wrong with him. He was exactly her type, if she had been looking. It wasn't that guys didn't find her attractive or interesting – she'd had many offers – it was just her previous involvement with men had made her cautious. They took her broken heart, mended it, made her feel on top of the world, and then tore her to shreds. Why was she always attracted to the wrong men? Why were the wrong men attracted to her? She was certain Mr Right was out there somewhere. However, he was going to have to find her because she had stopped looking months ago.

✺

Becky felt content that evening having just finished an important task well before the deadline. Part of her role as a marketing executive involved managing a large team, which meant working until exhausted and working overtime as she had nothing to go home for. Becky lived for the intense rush of her job.

The feeling she had left something behind festered. Reaching into her handbag, she rummaged through her belongings. Her credit card wallet was there, but her purse was in the bottom drawer of her desk.

This had never happened before, and the thought of telling the driver left her mouth dry. At first, the words wouldn't come, so she spoke louder, blurting it out.

"I'm sorry, but I think I've left my purse at work. I've money at home if you don't mind waiting."

He slammed on the brakes, right in the middle of the road, and then turned and glared at Becky.

"I've had about all I can take from liars and cheats. You think you can pull the wool over my eyes? Go on, get out!"

"I have money at home," she pleaded. "I'm not lying. I swear to you. Please, I don't know where I am. How am I supposed to get home?"

"That's not my bloody problem," he spat. "You should have thought about that before you tried to get a free ride. Now, get out of my cab before I come back there and drag you out."

She couldn't believe he would leave her stranded in a part of town she didn't know.

"You can't do this," she shouted. "I'm not getting out."

The driver turned off the engine and unclipped his belt while swearing profusely. Becky fumbled with the door handle and jumped out of the cab, stepping onto the otherwise deserted street. Speechless and stunned, she blew air into her hands as the cab pulled away. "Bollocks!" She cursed as she realized she'd left her mobile phone at the office as well.

She'd had an important meeting that morning and was dressed in high stiletto Jimmy Choos and her best D&G suit. She was certainly too dressed up to be walking around these streets.

Becky assumed she was heading into the shopping area when the road changed from tarmac to cobblestone. She navigated the stones with care, not wanting to twist her ankle. Turning a corner, the shops came into view. The street was deserted, apart from the echo of nearing footsteps. She pictured two couples out for a romantic evening stroll but didn't have the courage to check.

Thankfully, she spotted a red telephone box. Becky quickened her pace. To her dismay, so did the sound of trailing footsteps. Fear took over, and she moved as fast as her designer skirt would allow.

She reached the shelter of the telephone box and grabbed the receiver. Her hands were shaking so badly she could hardly keep a grip, never mind dial a number.

Further panic struck her. She had no purse, but if the footsteps belonged to the couples she had envisioned, wouldn't they give her some change for the phone?

Turning around, she saw a group of youths loitering in a doorway opposite the phone box. They looked harmless enough, probably hanging out like they did every night, but she didn't like the look of the smirk on one boy's face. She turned her back on them and rummaged through her bag, feeling for the loose change at the bottom.

Amongst the obscene graffiti and call girl invitations, she found a number for a local cab firm on the half-melted, plastic information board. Dialling the number, she spoke to a sympathetic woman who couldn't believe a driver would do something like that, and she even advised Becky to sue them.

The dispatcher's voice gave Becky a sense of security, and she didn't want to put the phone down. She told her about the youths, and the woman advised her to stay in a well-lit part of the street, assuring her a cab was already on the way.

Five minutes later, Becky continued to hold the phone and nod her head, even though the other woman had hung up minutes before. She couldn't stay in the phone box much longer. One youth was standing right outside, giving her an impatient glare.

Slowly, she put the receiver down and made a point of rummaging through her bag. Becky slipped out of the phone box and walked down the street at a confident, steady pace. She wanted to appear as if she knew where she was going, but she couldn't stray too far; the taxi could arrive at any moment, and she couldn't afford to miss it. More importantly, she didn't want to wander off too far and get lost.

It was a nightmare. All she wanted to do was get home, put her feet up, and forget the night had ever happened.

Behind her, the youths talked and laughed amongst themselves.

Becky stopped at a dress shop and looked in the window, feigning interest.

Instead of walking away as she'd hoped, they had the nerve to stand directly behind her. The five boys talked in high-pitched voices, acting as though they were interested in the dresses, causing more snorted laughter.

Becky didn't feel like laughing, and she didn't feel frightened. What she felt was anger, so she turned around and confronted them. "What's your problem?" she said, surprised her voice didn't shake.

"We're just wondering wha' a broad like you is doing 'round 'ere. You lost or some'fing?"

Becky guessed the lad was about fifteen. Claustrophobia overwhelmed her as they stepped forward, surrounding her. She couldn't see the street ahead and didn't know if the taxi was waiting.

"Not that it is any of your business, but I'm meeting my husband. Now, if you don't mind, get out of my way."

Becky pushed past them. A hand gripped her shoulder, and she spun around. In one quick move, she kneed the boy in the groin and ran, unfortunately, in the opposite direction to where she'd arranged for the taxi to pick her up. Desperate to lose the boys, Becky dived into a nearby alley.

Passage to Tsinia

FALDOR AND PARCER WITNESSED WITH interest the encounter between the woman they knew as Thya and the young humans. Could it be that they would not have to carry out the task themselves? Could the humans want to destroy her also?

"Darthorn will be interested in this hostile land, Parcer."

"With certainty, Faldor. Only I am ashamed to reveal I feel a little regretful about her."

Faldor turned to face his friend. "How so?"

"I pity anything hunted down, especially by a different species."

"I will not reiterate your remark. Darthorn would not condone this opinion, yet I do comprehend your thought. Come, let us not remain. Perhaps the humans fail in their task. I desire to conclude with haste and return to Senx. I do not find this atmosphere agreeable and feel the air is choking me. If we ever revisit, we will bear breathing resources."

They watched Becky dive into a narrow passage. Moments later, the foolish young humans ran past it.

Good, Faldor thought. Eager for the kill. He enjoyed his work, which had unfortunately slackened off. Taking out his primitive weapon, he looked at it with uncertainty. Were these strange metal objects able to destroy Thya's being?

The first time Faldor had pressed the mechanism, it had given off a loud noise and caused him to drop it to the ground, leaving his hand vibrating. After a couple of attempts, he understood how to hold the weapon and learnt how to target an object. He would do whatever his master commanded and bestow his existence to the cause. Only was it in error to feel pity for Thya?

She is unknown to her past, her powers, and who she truly is. She is an innocent, and yet if she is permitted to live, she would destroy Master. Whether I feel regretful for Thya or not, my master has given the order to have her breath removed, and I dare not fail in this unwanted task.

Becky glanced down the street. It looked deserted, but could she risk being out in the open? It was nice and wide and lit by streetlamps, but still daunting. What choice did she have though? She had to find another pay phone, ring a cab, and get as far away from this horrid place as she could. She took a deep breath and walked forward.

As she neared the bottom of the alley, a man stepped out in front of her and blocked her path. Becky jumped back with a cry.

The man held out his hands in a harmless gesture. "All is well," he spoke in haste. "I am not here to harm you, Thya. I have been sent to aid you."

"I'm a black belt in karate and these" – she waved her arms about – "are dangerous weapons."

The man chuckled.

"Who is Thya?" She waited for an answer.

Becky studied him. There was something friendly and warm about him, familiar even. Like herself, he was overdressed in his dark grey three-piece suit. He was elderly – Becky guessed in his sixties – so maybe it was his age that made her feel safe, He looked harmless enough; it was his words that didn't make sense. They unnerved her.

"'Tis urgent we depart," he told her. "We do not have duration—"

A shot rang out, echoing through the passageway between the buildings.

The man's face turned grave. "If you do not depart with me, Thya, you will cease to exist!"

Before she could question who this Thya was

again, Becky heard hurried footsteps rushing towards them. She stared at the man as he urged her to take his hand.

"Come with me," he begged.

She had two choices: She could leave with the strange man or face her attackers. She favoured the former. Grabbing hold of his hand, they ran down the remainder of the alley and turned right.

Farther along, they turned left and found garages on both sides of a lengthy road.

Becky watched as the man's eyes widened as two identically dressed men rounded the corner with guns drawn.

As she spun around, she noticed a garage door left partly open. Becky pointed to the door. The old man nodded and crawled underneath, pulling her in with him.

She took deep breaths to calm herself and was glad for a moment of rest.

"Who are you?" she finally asked her Samaritan.

Becky felt sure he wasn't going to harm her, and he was just helping her out of a dangerous situation. One she couldn't fathom how she'd gotten into.

"I am named Salco. That is all you require at present." He raised a finger to his lips. "Be silent."

Both listened for the sound of running feet. Becky squeezed her eyes shut and prayed the attackers wouldn't notice their makeshift sanctuary. To her relief, the footsteps became a distant echo. Silently they waited, and after a few moments more, Salco slid under the garage door to check if it was safe for them to leave. He glanced both ways then signalled to Becky.

"I trust I have proven that I am not here to harm you. You are obligated to depart with me now. 'Tis no longer safe for you here."

Although she still didn't understand what he meant, by it not being safe anymore, she didn't have a clue what to do next and so took his outstretched hand. They ran back the way they had come. Becky did her best to keep up; however, for an old man, he was extremely fit. She soon lost her footing and fell to the ground, grazing her knee.

"Are you well?" he asked in alarm. "I was too hasty. This will not do. Are you well?"

The concern was flattering, yet a little over the top. "I'm fine. Let's get out of here, okay?"

As she stood and brushed off the dust from her clothes, Salco remained on the spot and stared at her.

"Why are you looking at me like that?"

"Pardon me. I do not mean to. I just… I cannot believe I stand in your presence."

Before she had time to ask him more questions, shots ricocheted off the walls around them.

Salco grasped her hand. "With haste!"

They raced down an alley.

Her heart jumped when she saw another open door. Salco practically dragged her into the abandoned warehouse, only releasing his grip after he shut the door. He used three crates sitting beside the wall to bolster it. They looked heavy, yet he moved them as if they weighed nothing.

His attention was fixated on the door, but when he turned around to look at her, horror spread across his face. He ran to her and paced franticly.

"You are damaged? 'Tis not forewarned. He continued to pace before her, wringing his hands. "What have I done?"

Becky didn't understand what he meant until she felt a stabbing pain in her side. She looked down to see her blouse soaked with blood. She pressed her hand against the wetness and gasped as it came away red. She didn't recall getting hit, but the sight of blood made her swoon and she slid down the wall, her legs splayed.

Salco knelt beside her, his eyes never leaving the spreading stain, and took her hand into his. "I will transport you to the healer. Valcan is the only one who can aid you."

"Valcan?" she whispered. Strength sapped from her body, and her head slumped forward.

The Changlins

PREPARATIONS WERE UNDERWAY FOR Thya's arrival. They had been expecting her since the writing of the first Oracle long ago. Omad, the head of the council, made sure everyone knew of her coming, for it was his task to prepare his people for the arrival of their princess. He'd left strict instructions that no one witness the arrival or approach until he had conversed with her himself. It was his duty to inform Thya who she was and of her destiny.

He felt anxious and nervous, but not for himself. Tsinia was his home, but to an outsider, a human, it might seem like a mystical, dreamlike place. How was he to make her understand? Would she listen, and, most importantly, would she believe him? Too much was at stake. He could not fail. The fate of Tsinia lay in his hands.

Omad stretched and rubbed the back of his neck as he pondered over his revised speech. Would it be too much for her to take in? He nodded his head, feeling happy with his decision to inform her of her true identity. Telling her about the prophecy could wait. He didn't relish that task.

Omad looked around the gold leaf-covered throne room. Soon, she would take her rightful place among her people, and they would once again have a ruler, removing the burden from the Tsinian council. He clenched his trembling, clammy hands. He had been preparing for this moment since being appointed head long ago.

His election had been a cause for celebration, the start of planned preparations to bring their queen home.

The council comprised of twelve elected Tsinians, those held in the highest regard. The head of the council was seated centrally in a semicircle of chairs, his seat raised so there could be no doubt of who was in charge. Tsinian business was held in the Escos on the border of their land. Meetings were not open, and only by appointment could citizens address the council.

Omad sighed, remembering the feast held in his

honour, the one time he had felt truly scared. The nomination was in recognition of his work, yet to be chosen for a task with repercussions that could destroy Tsinia's existence was something he wished hadn't been entrusted to him.

There was much excitement and discussion about how Thya would become the saviour of them all, how her return would cause the warlord's demise.

The Tsinians lived by the words of the Oracle, and although there was no indication of how Thya would save Tsinia from Darthorn's domination, the people felt as though their troubles were over. They were so confident that for the first time in the history of their great land an Oracle was ignored.

Omad shivered as he recalled Athron confronting the council with the latest reading. Were they wrong to ignore the warning?

The Oracles were written upon ancient scrolls. It was a riddle that only a Zenith could interpret, for it was they who wrote them. The generations of Zeniths were male who were born with the gift of Sight.

Omad remembered being awoken from his sleep by a very anxious Athron. He demanded the council assemble at once, and, as a Zenith and valued Tsinian, Omad took the urgency seriously.

"I would not have removed you from your slumber if I did not consider this to be of consequence," Athron announced when the council had convened.

"Continue," Omad said.

"The Oracle proclaims a warning."

Omad, suddenly wide awake, frowned. "Good Athron, decipher."

Athron nodded and unrolled the scroll. "Not all will come to pass, and though the saviour will return, she will not be delivered."

The council whispered among themselves.

"Rephrase," Omad said.

"Our lady will return, but she will not be who you expect. The matrimony will not be entered upon. There is no alliance. For 'tis written, so it will be."

"Nonsense," Tasarc retorted. "Tis ludicrous. The alliance is established. All that is required is our lady's sign."

"And what if she does not sign?" Athron said.

Omad rose from his seat. There was silence. "I sympathise with your anxiety, Athron. We all are concerned with our future. Nonetheless, as our good friend Tasarc remarked, the alliance will proceed. As for our lady not receiving us, tis her duty as princess of Tsinia to aid her kinsmen. I am confident that once she returns, all will be well. Do not distress." Omad then reseated.

Athron continued, "I pray you are accurate. The fact is the Oracles have never been unjust. Do not shut your eyes to the truth."

Athron had spoken out of turn, and Omad had to show strength in front of his peers. He stood abruptly from his seat. "'Tis proper you have brought this to our attention. You will retire," he ordered.

Only Athron did not turn to leave. "You sight only what you want. Free your eyes!"

"Silence," Omad growled.

The council gasped.

"Dare you judge me? I will not justify myself to you." He then lowered his voice. "Athron, I hold you in the highest esteem. Be assured we will review the Oracle and rule on the correct outcome. Depart – now."

Athron left, yet Omad knew he would not let it rest. He learnt of Athron's visit to Nimas, the Wise One. Who also agreed that the reader of Oracles had misinterpreted? Twice more Athron had visited Omad begging for him to be taken seriously.

Now, as Omad waited for his princess's arrival, he regretted treating Athron disrespectfully. Should he have taken heed? Only it did not make sense. If the Tsinian's alliance with the Senxs did not result in peace, what was Thya's calling?

The Senxs had been enemies with the Tsinians for centuries. The current warlord, Darthorn, was the worst Senx to ever rule the land. Controlling his kinsmen with dark magic, his strength and power seemed to grow every moon.

We won't be able to resist much longer. Our final hope is the return of our long-lost princess, heir of Tsinia.

Athron's late father, Ganard, was the Zenith who received the vision that told that she would return to her land and save Tsinia from its impending doom. The Oracle never specified how she was to liberate Tsinia, so the council took it upon themselves to come up with a solution. They decided she would make an alliance with the Senx then patted themselves on the back for coming up with such an easy resolution.

Darthorn had readily agreed to the alliance, after adding one special condition.

But what if Athron was just? What if she did not sign the treaty? Could there be another way from which Thya could deliver them? Omad's thoughts were interrupted when Zarc entered the Escos.

"It has begun," Zarc said excitedly.

Omad hurried to the portal's entrance.

He hoped he was correct in sending Salco. It was a simple enough task. All Salco had to do was contact and persuade her to return with him. How hard could that be? As he waited, perspiration trickled down his face.

The bright light of the orb appeared. Omad glanced around, ensuring no one else was close by. His heart raced; he'd never felt so nervous. A shadow appeared through the light, but he could only make out one shape. Where was she? Had Salco failed in his mission? Then, through the mist, Salco appeared, carrying the seemingly lifeless body of their princess.

Omad gasped. "What has occurred?"

"It was not in my control."

"This cannot be. How could you permit this to transpire?"

Omad walked to Salco, every step heavy. He felt drained, as if there was no hope left.

"She has breath," Salco told him.

Those three glorious words brought Omad back. "Then hope remains. Valcan holds an understanding of what can be done."

Hastily, they left for the Tora, Valcan's dwelling.

"Inform me on what occurred. Declare all," Omad commanded as they hurried.

"'Tis not my failing, Omad. I swear. There were Senxs upon Earth, ahead of my arrival. They possessed weapons. I had naught to defend us, and I was not informed of their coming. I was not aware of a threat."

"I appreciate this, Salco. I am concerned, though. How did the Senxs discover our plans? Is there an informer among us? No… no, there cannot be." He paused. "You are not to converse on this. Understood?"

"'Tis, Omad, and I pray to the Changlins that she will survive. I would bestow my existence if it would benefit the princess."

Omad deemed it wrong to comfort Salco. He had failed in his mission, whatever the reason. Nonetheless, Omad would have to answer for Salco's mistake.

He took the princess from Salco's arms. "Depart at once to the council, relate to them on what has occurred, stay silent about the informer and, Salco… bestow hope upon them."

"It will be done."

Valcan was just sitting down to eat when Omad burst through the door. For a moment, he was stunned by the sudden appearance of his friend, more so when he saw the pale human in his arms. Valcan noted how tired and haggard Omad looked. He stood abruptly, rushing towards him, and he took Thya and carried her to his healing room.

"Leave me," Valcan ordered.

Omad left, but not before giving instructions for Valcan to notify him if there was news.

The only way Omad could help Thya now was to pray to the Changlins. Pray that Valcan would find the strength to save her.

Valcan healed with the use of his gift and needed solitude to concentrate. He did not allow anyone to observe him at work. He'd never seen damage to a human before, but Thya wasn't human; she was Bora.

He didn't know if it was in his power to save her. Nonetheless, he closed his eyes, placed his hands over her womb, and began the healing process.

Omad needed time to meditate and ask for guidance, so he headed for the Plecky.

How could he have allowed this to happen?

After entering the building, he knelt before the five small monoliths known as the Changlins. They stood upon a square pillar and were arranged in a circle. A bright light radiated from within. It pulsed like a heartbeat, and, in a sense, that was what it was, the heart of Tsinia. Each sacred stone represented one of the elements: earth, fire, water, air and spirit, the essences of Tsinia's survival. It was said the stones contained power, and as long as the Tsinians possessed the Changlins, they would continue to possess their very special gifts. In paying homage to the Changlins, they believed that in return, the Changlins would protect their land. They were treated as an icon, and though the Changlins never answered, the Tsinians never stopped praying.

He stared at the stones as he knelt in silent prayer. Was his eyesight playing a trick on him? It seemed the light within the stones was softening, fading even. Omad could not believe he was witnessing the worst of omens for Tsinia. It filled him with terror to think the blessed light could extinguish before his eyes.

He sat stunned. What was making the light fade? Could it be related to Thya's arrival? To her lack of wellbeing? The only conclusion he could come up with was that her soul was somehow connected to the stones.

If that were possible, then she was indeed an exceptional Tsinian. Alas, it also meant that Thya's internal power was fading. Omad squeezed his eyes shut, begging the Changlins to save her. He opened his eyes and gazed intently at the stones, hoping that one word, uttered from his heart, would strengthen the light. He also prayed that Valcan would have the power to revive her. Was his gift enough?

Hearing footsteps heading towards him, he turned and stood to meet Salco.

After learning of Omad's theory, he watched Salco fall to his knees and his face pale.

Surely, Darthorn could not win so easily. Alas, the light still flickers, and it seems likely that our hope and saviour will lose her breath.

Valcan had done what he could, using all his knowledge and skill. In fact, he had worked on Thya for such a long time that he felt completely drained of energy. His legs felt shaky, and he leaned against the stone wall to keep from falling. If he were to help her any further, he would have to get his own strength back. He required food and left the room in search of something to eat.

Darthorn's messengers had returned from Earth and were telling their master about the strange land and what had occurred.

"You are confident that she was damaged, Faldor?"

"Tis assured, master. How badly could not be sighted. Pacer comprehends those primitive weapons better than I."

"And you state the humans were also targeting Thya?" Darthorn inquired.

"Tis so, master. Though I sighted not weapons, they are hostile people."

"Interesting," remarked Darthorn.

Kovon had heard enough, and entered. He walked straight up to the warlord, knelt on one knee, and kissed Darthorn's hand. "I retain information from Jakar, Father. Thya has entered Tsinia, though she is gravely hurt. Tis doubtful she will survive. Jakar informs me that Valcan, their healer, is with her and has been for some duration."

Darthorn turned to his son. "This is cheering to discover. So, the mission was a success. Absent of Thya, I will persist in my plan to rule Tsinia. Once I possess the power of the Changlins naught will prevent me."

Darthorn addressed his messengers. "You have done well and will be rewarded. Depart."

Faldor and Pacer turned to leave.

Before they could leave, Kovon called out. "Is she… is she everything they express?" he asked.

"I had sight for only a brief instant," Pacer answered. "She is ordinary, like the entire human race. I did not note any uniqueness."

Kovon dismissed them with a wave of this hand, leaving father and son alone.

Darthorn looked questionably at Kovon. "You do not exhibit delight with this information. Why not?"

"I have perceived much of this Thya," he spat the word out. "Tis a pity I will not sight her. I wonder — does she appear as I imagine?"

"Tis possible you will still encounter her — if she survives."

"Let us hope she does not. Father, I will withdraw, for I am eager to receive further information from Jakar." He bowed before departing.

Oh, I do hope she survives. I desire for my father to take control of the Changlins and enslave the Tsinians. Oh, what sight it would be, their princess Thya down on her knees in front of the Lord of Senx.

Kovon never interfered with his father's battles,

preferring to remain in the background. Even so, he secretly observed his father's plans with interest.

Knowing that one day Senx would become his, and if by then they had conquered Tsinia, it would make him one of the most powerful warlords of all time. He had heard much about Thya from their spy, Jakar, and especially looked forward to the other half of his father's plan: that he would remove the last obstacle from Darthorn's domination and kill Thya himself.

Why should the Senxs agree to an alliance? What was in it for them? They needed to get rid of Thya before they could control Tsinia, and the best way to do that was to get her on their territory. Only, why was he thinking so far ahead when it looked doubtful they would ever meet. Jakar had told Kovon about the Oracle predicting there would be no alliance, thanks to his father's plan to have her killed before she learnt of her gifts or even the existence of Tsinia. Pity, he'd looked forward to making her beg for mercy. There was still a chance she would endure. Should that happen, he wanted to be prepared.

Kovon, too, had a gift, one that he used only when it suited him. Not even his father knew of his talents. He discovered his power at an early age and taught himself. It worked better if they didn't suspect anything.

He could have anything he wanted – when he wanted.

Darthorn looked out of his window, the size of which covered one side of the great chamber. Tsinia looked so vulnerable from up there.

The Senxs lived on top of a huge, dark mountain in dome-shaped dwellings coloured grey and black. Situated in the middle of them was Darthorn's magnificent abode. His dome was three times the size of the others and was covered with gold.

Senx could not be seen from Tsinia, only the monstrous, black mountain it sat upon. However, from Darthorn's chamber, the whole of Tsinia could be viewed. It looked small and meek, easy to destroy, which, unfortunately, wasn't true as he had found out numerous times.

Firstly, the Oracles prophesied most of his plans, so when an attack did come, his enemies were ready. With the amount of Tsinians possessing special gifts, it had so far been enough to prevent him from taking Tsinia, and together with the power of the Changlins, he'd never gotten close.

The Darkeye was a jet black, oval crystal housed in a cavern within the warrior's domain where only a warlord could enter. Certain death was promised to anyone else who tried. Should a warlord employ the evil Dark Force within, he would call on it and be given the price of payment before he could make use of that power.

He stood in thought, dwelling on the time he called on the Dark Force and sent a deadly mist upon them, one that should have wiped them out.

He had been shown the delicious effects of the mist. Starting with a shortness of breath, the victim would choke. Simultaneously, their eyes and nose would bleed. After vomiting blood, they would eventually succumb to suffocation. Oh, how he wanted to witness the effects, but, as always, the Tsinians were prepared. Jakar had related to him how only one gifted Tsinian had put an end to the poisonous cloud.

Unfortunately, every time Darthorn used the Dark Force, it cost him dearly in return. To receive the deadly mist, Darthorn sacrificed ten of his warriors to prove his loyalty to the dark side.

Having no special gifts of their own, the warlords of Senx used the Darkeye for guidance. It spoke to them, giving advice and direction. Only in desperate circumstances would they call upon the Dark Force. For the most part, Darthorn used the DarkEye for predictions.

The Eye told him of a special Ganty who was to be born, one who would eventually destroy him. He decided to kill the child the following Trill moon. and planned a surprise attack. As always, his plan had been prophesied, and the child was sent to a place of safety. In desperation and outrage, Darthorn had the king and queen killed, leaving Tsinia without a Ganty to rule them.

Salco was the first to see the stones flicker. He tapped Omad on the shoulder to get his attention. Omad opened his eyes and saw it for himself; the Changlins shone unsteadily, as if unsure what to do. Silently, Omad prayed; although, Salco spoke his feelings aloud. "Go on. You can do it. That is it. Slowly."

Omad smiled. Salco was talking to the Changlins as if they were two moons old. However, it seemed to be working. He had a difficult time stopping himself from joining in. Instead, he silently willed the stones' light to grow.

The glow strengthened, and the Changlins were as bright, if not brighter, than ever before. In delight, the Tsinians stood and hugged each other. Once composed, Omad left the Plecky and hurried towards the Tora in hopes Thya had recovered, as he was certain she had. Salco ran quietly behind.

Valcan unintentionally fell asleep. He woke a while later, and after fully regenerating his energy, he felt stronger than before. It took a few moments before the memory of Thya flooded back. Even before he reached her, he knew she was going to live. As soon as he walked into the room, he noticed her rosy, glossy skin. She had full red lips, and her cheekbones were more defined. However, what stood out the most was her long, silver hair that was notoriously associated with a Ganty. She was Tsinian; there was no doubt about it. Kneeling beside her, he positioned his hands an inch above her chest. He smiled, satisfied with his work. She was sleeping peacefully, and her skin looked radiant and healthy. He couldn't help but stare at his beautiful princess, and a tear rolled down his cheek. He felt proud he had the skill and power within him to heal her. Only…was this delicate flower really their saviour?

He had just sat down when he heard a frantic knocking on his door.

"Enter," Valcan said.

Salco and Omad stared at him questionably.

"Our lady is well?" Omad inquired.

"She is well and resting."

"Grant praise to the Changlins," Salco and Omad chorused.

"Salco, go to the council and inform them on our lady's wellbeing. Advise them I will appear shortly."

Salco bowed and then departed.

"To what extent will our lady slumber?"

"'Tis difficult to sense. At this moment, she is weak and requires relaxation."

"I grasp this. Nonetheless, I am compelled to converse with her as soon as I am able."

"I am aware of the urgency, Omad. However, I do not recommend this. She is not in a state to receive you. It would be unsafe to agitate her."

"I am confident you are just, Valcan. Swear to me the instant she wakes, send word. Not one is to converse with her prior to me."

"Your command is understood, Omad. I will dispatch word without delay."

Omad left the Tora in haste, knowing the council would be waiting to hear from him. He'd made a grave mistake sending Salco to retrieve the princess on his own. Omad was expected to be wise and foresee the unforeseen after all.

Becky woke from her sleep to find a sombre face looking down at her. She sat up in surprise. Her mouth hung open as she studied the strangely dressed man in front of her.

The blue tunic that clung to his lean, tall build, was tied around his waist with a plaited grass belt. A single binding of wild grass held his long, chestnut-coloured hair from his face. He had a stern appearance, with penetrating blue eyes and a short, yet bushy, beard. Becky assumed he was middle-aged, though not quite mature in years. Who was this strangely dressed man?

And, more importantly, where was she? She recalled the stranger who had stepped in front of her in the alleyway. Remembering what had happened, she looked down to where she'd been hurt and was surprised to find herself dressed in a green embroidered gown.

"Wow" She gasped. Her eyes opened wide.

Becky looked wildly around the strange-shaped room; she'd never seen anything quite like it. She was dreaming. Yes, that was it. It was all a dream. The shooting, the Samaritan – what did he say his name was? Zalco? She had assumed she would wake up at any moment in her own bed. It may have started as a nightmare, but it had turned into a pleasant dream.

When she turned her head to check out her surroundings, a wisp of silver hair fell on her chest. It was the first time her hair had changed colour, and she jumped off the bed to take a good look at herself in the mirror across the room.

Her mouth gaped. She looked like a fairy from A Midsummer Night's Dream. Maybe that's who she was. Titania, queen of the fairies.

"Wonderful," she said.

Suddenly remembering the strange man in the room, she finally acknowledged him. "Hello. Who are you?"

Valcan remembered Omad's words, bowed, and quickly departed without a reply.

"How rude," Becky mumbled.

She returned her attention to the mirror, enjoying the unusual realism of the dream. She was eager to check out her surroundings, take in every sight and sound, savour every moment. She hoped when she awoke she would have something to help her remember this unusual dream.

Valcan found Omad standing in front of the councillors. He wondered how Omad felt, being on the other side for a change. Many a time, Valcan had been in that position, and he hadn't liked the feeling at all. From their raised voices, Valcan sensed the meeting wasn't going too well. He coughed to gain their attention. He watched as relief washed over Omad's face.

So as to not look like he was hiding in the shadows, Valcan stepped into the centre of the room and nodded respectively to the councilmen. There was no need to speak to Omad, for he looked eager to leave the councilmen's scrutiny. Valcan turned to follow his friend when one of the members called out to him. He walked towards the addressing star in the middle of the floor.

"I am your servant as always," Valcan greeted.

"Announce to us, Valcan. What is our lady likened to?"

What a question to ask him. Were they asking if

she could liberate Tsinia? He couldn't answer that. Was she beautiful? Certainly, there was no doubt in his mind. Only their question had many hidden meanings, and they were waiting patiently for an answer.

"She is a Ganty."

With their curiosity satisfied, they signalled for him to leave. Valcan soon caught up with Omad.

"Did you converse with her?" Omad asked.

"I did not. Although she is eager for dialogue."

"Is that so?"

Valcan left him at the door, knowing that he wanted to speak to her alone. Omad entered the Tora and found Thya walking around the room looking at all the possessions. He stood patiently until she noticed his presence.

"Hello," she said.

Becky put down the trinket and stared at him.

She watched as he studied her in return. He stood up straight, took a deep breath, and then smiled at her.

"You remind me of someone," she said

He laughed, which made Becky smile. "I am named Omad."

"Hello, Omad. I'm Becky."

"Nay, you are not," he declared. "Come, I have something to convey, and you would be more comfortable being seated."

That was the hard part over. All he had to do now

was convince her of who she really was. He cleared his throat. "You are named Thya. You are the princess of Tsinia, sadly the last of the Ganties. You were returned to your homeland as a result of an ancient Oracle that prophesied that you would deliver your kinsmen from Darthorn, the warlord of Senx." He stopped then to catch his breath. "More will be clarified to you in the coming future."

Omad stared as though waiting for her reaction. She burst out laughing. "Oh, how wonderful. I've always wanted to be a princess."

Omad sighed in relief.

"So, when do I get to meet my prince?"

Omad frowned. "How are you acquainted with Prince Kovon? Who has conversed with you?"

"Nobody has conversed with me," she exaggerated his strange choice of words. "It's obvious, isn't it? Every princess has a Prince Charming, but he must be handsome and a real gentleman if I am to do this right."

"Right?"

"Well, yes, this is a beautiful dream. I don't want an ugly prince, do I?" She laughed.

Omad gasped, and she stepped back.

"Thya, tis not an illusion. You are awake. Tis not your inventiveness; tis reality. You are required to grasp the importance of why you were returned. Your citizens await your aid."

"If this is… reality," Becky said, "then as your

princess, you can't keep me locked up in this room. I can walk out of here this very minute."

"If that is what you desire. You are not a felon; you are not even a guest. Tis your home. You are the rightful heir. Just the same, I suggest you dress in the proper attire, lest you chance upon your subjects."

Becky looked down at the beautiful gown she was wearing. "What's wrong with this?"

"That garment is for resting." Omad chuckled. "I will summon your attendant. She will be certain you are suitably attired."

Deciding to play along, she waved him away.

"This is amazing," she squealed. Didn't every girl dream of meeting their Prince Charming? It was such a vivid, peculiar dream that it was almost frighteningly real.

A gentle tap on the door got her attention. "Come in."

A lovely brunette girl entered. She wore a dull-coloured robe with a grass belt, and her long, brown hair was neatly tied back. A cream silk dress hung over her arm. The young Tsinian curtsied before approaching Becky. Taking Becky's hand, she led her to a stool next to the mirror. She watched carefully as the girl began to dress her hair.

"You're very quiet," Becky said. "You either can't

speak or have been ordered not to. It doesn't matter which. So, this place is called Sidinia?"

"Tsinia," corrected the girl before she quickly covered her mouth.

Becky turned around. "Ah! So, you do speak." She laughed. "It's okay; I won't tell the old man. What's your name?"

"Kezar."

"How old are you, Kezar?"

"Old? I do not comprehend."

"How many years of age are you?"

"I do not recognise what you mean." Kezar bent her head, as if she were ashamed of not being able to understand.

Becky realised she would have to explain herself if she was to make Kezar cheerful again. "Okay, when you are born, you live one day, which makes you one day old. When you have lived eight years, you are eight years old. Understand?"

"I believe so," Kezar replied as she continued dressing Becky's hair. She braided the sides and pinned them to the back of Becky's head while she let the rest of the hair hang loose. Kezar stood Becky up and began undressing her.

"So," Becky repeated, "how old are you?"

The girl stopped what she was doing and considered. "I am not acquainted with this. We do not embrace year or day."

"Really? That's so weird. Well, I'd say you look about eighteen."

"You will not sight many Tsinians younger than I," Kezar said.

Becky was curious. "Oh, why is that?"

Kezar explained. "When we are born, we are an infant for a short while, a day, I believe you name it. Then on our second birthday, we become at an age" – Kezar checked to see she had said the word correctly, and Becky nodded – "at an age when we are intelligent enough to master the code and arts. Tis a short while since I first commenced."

"Are you telling me there are no children here?"

"Tis true. I beg of you; do not convey to Omad that I have conversed with you. Tis not my place."

"This is incredible. You know, the worst thing about having a child is the dirty nappies," she joked.

Kezar looked at Becky blankly.

"Oh, never mind, you wouldn't understand."

"I have concluded," announced Kezar. "You are prepared."

Becky stood up and admired herself in the mirror. She certainly looked like a princess. Her hair was beautifully pinned, and the silk dress reminded her of a Roman toga. The front hung modestly and tied around her waist was a gold coloured rope.

She sighed deeply, wishing she could look this way when she awoke. Men would fall at her feet. She twirled around, swishing the long skirt from side to side.

"You are beautiful, Thya. You have the appearance of a true Ganty."

"What's a Ganty?"

"'Tis the title of your ancestors. All rulers of Tsinia are named Ganty. Sadly, you are the conclusion. Tis why you have been returned."

Becky ignored Kezar's last comment and walked towards the door.

"Nay, Thya, we are compelled to remain in the Tora We cannot depart unaccompanied."

"Am I your princess?"

"With certainty, only—"

"Then I command we leave – now."

Kezar curtsied and ran ahead to open the door.

Becky made a mental note to make an appointment with her hairdresser when she woke up. Silver highlights and hair extensions would suit her, and she would certainly get noticed around town.

Becky stopped, stunned by the view in front of her.

Her lungs filled with the scent of flowers and wonderful perfumes, and the air smelt so sweet and pure. She stared in amazement at the magnificent sky. The silver-and-blue cloudless sky and suns – or were they moons? – two of them, one full and one crescent-shaped.

She was in a forest, that much was apparent. Tall,

dark trees lined the open path, only they were no ordinary trees. Each thick trunk had a small wooden door painted in bright colours on it. Most of them were closed. However, Becky saw one that was ajar and glimpsed a set of wooden steps that must surely wind inside the trunk, as though they had been carved out of the tree itself. Colourful flowers and plants bloomed around the tree. Each small garden looked well kept, as if dearly loved and tended to.

Becky finally stepped out of the Tora and found the ground to be soft. Like all Tsinians, she was barefooted. The forest floor was covered in wood chips and crisp, golden leaves that crunched as she walked on them. Becky gazed at her strange surroundings.

To her immediate left, she saw two strangely shaped grey buildings. They looked as if they could have been made out of clay. To her right was another, but it was much larger than the other one. The rest of the forest looked absent of buildings. The routes to the buildings were clearly defined by a well-trodden path. Apart from the obvious tracks, the remaining forest was rural and wild, just as nature intended. Without another thought, Becky headed in the direction of the two buildings.

Alkazar had been given the task of tutoring Thya in the arts. The only gift he possessed was teaching his fellow Tsinians how to unleash and control their special powers. Not everyone had a gift, but those who did possessed varying skills that were passed from one bloodline to the next. Like the Zeniths, they had the gift of Sight and could foretell future occurrences.

The rulers of Tsinia, the Ganties, possessed the gift of Flite, and they could move objects with their mind. It was a difficult gift to unleash and would take a lot of work to teach Thya. To make his task harder, Thya should have been trained from her second birthday. Only now, she was to come to him at twenty-four Earth years. How was he supposed to teach her at that age?

To add to this undertaking, Athron had urged him to train Thya as quickly as possible. He told Alkazar about the last Oracle, and Alkazar took the threat seriously. He had studied Thya's world so could communicate with her better than others. He understood how she lived and about human emotions.

During the last few tril moons, the name "Thya" had been spoken in every conversation, and he was eager to meet the woman to see if she was all she was supposed to be.

Alkazar was busy studying when he heard Omad calling him. It was unusual for anyone to shout up to the dwellings, and he wondered why Omad did not come up to talk in person. It had to be important, so he put the book down, walked to the wooden balcony, and leaned over.

"Alkazar, a moment," Omad called up.

Without hesitation, Alkazar bounded down the stairs to meet him. "I am your servant," he greeted breathlessly.

Omad told him of Thya's attack and of her recovery, along with his concern that she had insisted it was just a dream. "Tis why I require your assistance. Your acquaintance is superior to anyone else. I entrust to you to bring about her change and compel her to grasp the situation."

Alkazar was taken back by the request. "I am honoured you have chosen me. Only if it is so prudent to influence an opinion onto our lady, would not it be superior for her to discover for herself who she is?"

"I concur," Omad answered. "Alas, we do not possess the duration to tarry. I anticipate communication from Darthorn shortly, and our lady is required to be prepared to take her standing amidst her subjects. I recognise you have a burdensome task ahead, and what I am requesting from you may seem unfeasible. Nevertheless, it should be done."

Alkazar didn't need to think about it. Firstly, it was not prudent to refuse the council, and secondly, it seemed like an excellent opportunity to meet the princess.

"I will surrender my all to your command, Omad. Where will I chance upon our lady?"

"I am confident you will not fail, my friend. Come, we journey in unison."

"Do you not desire to visit your dwelling?" Kezar asked.

Becky turned to answer, but her vision blurred, almost as if she was looking at an illusion. It lasted only a few seconds, but even so, it scared her.

Kezar pointed to the largest of the four buildings.

"Not now," Becky said and continued to walk as though she knew where she was going. Something was pulling her towards one of the buildings, only she wasn't going against her will. Every step made her feel warm and content.

As she neared the Plecky, a chill crept over her, and she shuddered. Eager to shake off the strange feeling, she struck up a conversation. "Where do you live? I can't see any homes around here, apart from these four buildings," Becky signalled to them.

Kezar laughed. "We dwell up high."

Becky looked up, craning her neck in the direction Kezar pointed to. "Where? I can't see anything."

"Up high, within the ancient trees."

That was when Becky saw Tsinia. A whole city built within the trees and camouflaged by lush green leaves. Houses made of wood and straw were built between the sturdy branches of the ancient, giant trees. Each house looked similar in design and size, and every one of them had a charming wooden balcony. Yet what astounded Becky the most was the wooden rope bridges connecting each home, as though you could walk from one end of the treetops to the other. She looked around. There were hundreds of them, and she sensed a unity between the inhabitants. They trusted one another and had no enemies among them.

She noticed small heads peering down at her. Goosebumps prickled her arms. She had an awful feeling she wasn't dreaming, that she was wide awake and had somehow been here before.

"Are you well, my lady? You appear colourless," Kezar said.

"I'm fine. Just had a dizzy spell."

However, no matter how she tried to shake off the feeling, she couldn't get the déjà vu to pass. The forest closed in around her, stifling her breath.

"What is it, my lady? Is anything amiss?"

Becky felt the panic rise in her throat. Her heart pounded as though it would soon jump out of her chest, and she was gripped by a sudden fear that left her unable to move or speak.

Two Tsinian men approached.

While Alkazar stared at her with astonishment, Omad's face was scornful. "Kezar, I instructed you not to withdraw until my appearance. I was to accompany you both." He studied Becky's face. "My lady, you are not yet satisfactory. Return to the Tora with me, I beseech you."

"Can you hear that?" Becky whispered.

"I perceive naught," Omad replied.

"What is it you hear?" Alkazar asked gently.

She stared at Alkazar as the unknown force continued to pull her along. "Whispers… voices… they're getting louder. They're calling to me. Can you hear them?"

Becky pointed towards the smallest building. "Omad, what's in this building?"

"Why do you inquire such? Return with me, my lady. You are not yet able enough to be out of doors—"

"Permit her to continue to the Plecky, Omad. She is compelled to proceed," Alkazar said.

Becky continued to walk. "The voices are coming from inside. I must go to them."

Omad could not persuade her to leave with him and followed behind silently.

They were only a few steps away from the entrance when Becky swooned. Alkazar ran to her side and held her up.

Omad tutted loudly. "I declare that you are unwell. You will rest?"

"I'm okay." She leaned on Alkazar for support.

"What is drawing you to the Plecky, my lady?" Alkazar asked. "What is so significant about this place?"

"I don't know. I've no idea why I'm here. I just feel… I have to be. Does that make sense?"

As Omad opened the entrance to walk in, Alkazar rested his hand on his shoulder. "Nay, my friend, our lady will venture in solitude."

After the door had shut behind her, Omad sent Kezar to ready the princess's dwelling, certain that food and a hot drink would be required.

"Clarify, Alkazar. Why do you perceive you recognise our lady's actions?"

"There is something exceptional about Thya, yet I am not certain what it is. A powerful force surrounds her, and I am keen to gain an understanding of what this signifies. There is a subtle aura that glows around her. Tis silver in colour. I am not surprised she is drawn to the Changlins"

Omad told Alkazar about the fading light of the Changlins and his belief that they called to her, though he could not understand why.

"This does not amaze me. I sense an intense connection between herself and the Changlins. She is a unique Ganty. I am excited to instruct her and curious to discover how powerful her ability is."

"Perseverance, my friend, we have yet to persuade her to accept her destiny."

"It could pass that we will not be forced to," Alkazar said as he looked at the closed door.

As soon as she had entered the Plecky, she felt she needed to kneel in front of oblong shaped monoliths as she stared not knowing what she was waiting for, again she felt another urge, this time it was to close her eyes. The moment her eyelids shut, she saw and spoke to her mother and father, the late rulers of Tsinia. Whether they were spirits, or a forgotten memory, it didn't matter to her. She believed every word she was told.

It seemed as though they had been waiting for an eternity when she finally emerged from the Plecky. Her face was pale and wet. Tears rolled down her cheek.

They remained silent until she was ready to speak.

"I have been given awareness of who I am. I am acquainted with who my mother and father were. I understand that I am not dreaming. It is clear to me now."

Omad sighed deeply.

Alkazar observed Thya as Omad ranted on about

how thrilled he was that she had accepted her fate and how happy her subjects would be.

Thya wasn't listening. She was trying to comprehend what the Changlins had told her. She didn't feel like herself. It was as if she was there but wasn't.

"I need to lie down. Will you excuse me?"

Omad ceased his chattering.

"Certainly. Kezar has prepared food and drink for you in your dwelling."

"Permit me to escort our lady," Alkazar offered.

"'Tis acceptable." Omad smiled. "I will provide the council with the revelation. Our conflicts will finally be concluded. We will stage a festival in honour of your homecoming. Does this cheer you, my lady? It will be a marvellous introduction to your subjects."

"Err… yes."

"Wonderful!"

Alkazar watched him leave then turned to Thya. "Take hold of my arm, princess, for I am confident your contact with the Changlins has drained most of your strength. Lean on me for support if you wish."

Thya smiled weakly.

They walked most of the way in silence. However, upon reaching her dwelling, Alkazar could no longer hold his tongue. "I can only imagine how you are feeling, Thya, I—"

"What is your name?"

"Alkazar, I—"

"Well, Alkazar, you couldn't possibly imagine how I feel because I'm not sure myself. I don't particularly want to talk about it, if that's all right with you."

"With certainty; however, I will express myself."

Thya stopped walking and glared at him, but it did not deter him from speaking his mind.

"You have come upon the realisation of who you are, and I believe this is overwhelming to you. I suggest you disregard all of this for the present. Do not reflect on what will come. Relax and sleep. Do not dwell too much on the past; exist in the present."

Thya smiled. She understood his words better than anything anyone else had said so far. "I thank you for the kind words, Alkazar. However, if you don't mind, I would like to be left alone."

"Certainly. We will encounter again at the festival. Rest well, my lady." He bowed then left.

The door to her new home was open, so Thya walked into the narrow hallway. She was met with a choice of three doors. The one to the left and right were both closed. The third door, situated at the far end of the corridor, was slightly ajar. A light shone from within, and Thya could make out shadows. Knowing that someone was inside, she approached the room cautiously.

She entered to find Kezar and two others preparing a table. When they saw her standing there, they stopped what they were doing and curtsied. One of the two, a plump, rosy-cheeked Tsinian, spoke enthusiastically.

"'Tis an honour to attend to you."

Thya forced a smile.

"We have developed a meal we believe you will relish."

The other Tsinian pulled out a chair and gestured for her to sit.

"Thank you. I hope you don't think I am rude, but do you mind leaving me alone?"

The two maids looked towards Kezar, puzzled. Kezar signalled for them to leave, which they did promptly, and then turned to follow them.

"Not you, Kezar. Please, stay."

Even though she wanted to be on her own, she needed someone to talk to. "Sit beside me."

"How may I serve you?" Kezar asked.

"You will serve me well by being a friend."

Kezar nodded.

Thya looked around the room, a humble place elegantly decorated with modest furniture. Certainly, it was more elaborate than the Tora. She sighed and looked down at the carved wooden bowl before her. It contained a bright orange liquid. She played absentmindedly with the wooden spoon, stirring the liquid while in deep thought.

"'Tis satisfying. Sample it." The sound of Kezar's voice shook Thya from her fog. "Grenko produced this for you. We are led to believe that humans delight in this strange food."

The word 'humans' gave Thya goose pimples. "Tell me, Kezar. Where is Tsinia? Am I on another planet? Another world? I mean, who are you?"

After a moment of thought, Kezar answered. "To us, Earth is another situation. A location not so unlike Tsinia. We are not dissimilar to humans." She quickly changed the subject, for it was not her place to speak of such things. "Thya, you ought to ingest if you are to retain your effectiveness."

Thya was so lost in thought she had forgotten about the food. She lifted the wooden spoon and sipped the warm, thin liquid. To her surprise, it tasted of tomatoes. It was… tomato soup. Thya's spirits rose slightly.

"You grow tomatoes here?"

"Grenko possesses the capability to cultivate and produce whatever he desires. He controls a gift we name Blooming," she announced proudly.

"Tell me more," Thya urged, amazed at what she was hearing.

"Tis not my standing, my lady. Alkazar is your mentor. He holds the undertaking of educating you about the arts."

"I command it." Thya smiled after using the word for the first time.

"Very well, my lady, if tis your command. Several Tsinians retain unique powers. I imagine you would name it as such. Alkazar is our mentor, and he tutors us on how to control and master our gifts."

"Like black magic?"

Kezar gasped. "Nay, my lady. We would never indulge with the dark side. Sorcery certainly."

"And does Alkazar have a special gift?"

Kezar paused before answering. "Nay, nor myself. The gifts are transmitted down specific generations."

Thya was scared to ask, yet she needed to know. "Does a Ganty… Do I possess powers?"

"With certainty. A Ganty is the most powerful. Tis guaranteed that you harbour a gift. Alas, Alkazar is required to prepare you initially."

"I… I have special powers," stuttered Thya. "This can't be. Please, don't tell me anymore." She couldn't hold it in any longer and sobbed uncontrollably. "I don't want this. I cannot take any more."

Kezar stared at her, bewildered.

Thya wiped her eyes. "I thought I was having a dream, that all this was a figment of my imagination. It's not, though, is it? It is real, and I don't want it to be."

Stunned by the revelation, Kezar went to comfort her.

"Tell them to take me back home, Kezar. I don't want any of this."

"Peace, my lady. All will be well."

"I don't belong here," Thya cried.

Kezar lifted Thya's chin and smiled sweetly at her.

"You will not be returned to Earth, my lady. Tsinia is your homeland, and it will remain so. You are compelled to recognise this."

Thya stopped crying and wiped her face. It seemed useless to talk. No one would understand.

Feeling weary and mentally exhausted, she stood and turned to Kezar. "I wish to lie down."

"'Tis fitting. I will accompany you to your chamber."

Kezar led her through the corridor to the door on the right and then opened it to display a large bedroom. Thya found herself looking at a four-poster bed three times the size of her own back on Earth. The bed was beautifully dressed in silk sheets. Six huge pillows lay across it. Muslin curtains hung from each bedpost.

A small, elegant dressing table was in the far corner, and there was an enormous wardrobe to her left. To her right was another closed door, and there was that fragrance again, a mixture of exotic fruit, flowers, and woodland spices.

"This room was formerly your mother and father's. It is currently yours," Kezar announced.

Thya didn't want to hear about a life that had never existed for her. "That will be all," she told Kezar.

"If you are in requirement of my assistance, summon me." Kezar pointed to the closed door. "It was to be your chamber. Would you care to view it?"

"Not now," Thya said impatiently and then

regretted her words. "I mean, I'm really tired. I'll have a look later."

"Very well, my lady. I hope your slumber is furnished with sweet visions."

Thya laid on the bed, too exhausted to undress. She fell into a deep sleep, even before her mind replayed the dreadful day. Only bad dreams disturbed her sleep, nightmare images of monsters and evil wizards. Then, just before she awoke, she dreamt of her real parents. She imagined – or saw, as it was so realistic – what her parents looked and sounded like. They spoke to her, telling her how much they loved her and how proud they were of who she had become. They told her how much it pained them to send her away and that it was because she had lived on Earth that she was different, yet so very special.

They warned her of bad times ahead and advised her to keep the strength of their love deep inside her.

⁂

While their princess slept, the villagers did what they did best and organised the festival. It was to be a feast of dancing and merriment. Everyone was enthusiastic, and laughter and drink flowed as they worked. It had been a long time since the Tsinian's last celebration.

The Festival

ALKAZAR TOLD HER TO RELAX AND NOT worry about the next day. Easy for him, Thya thought. He hadn't been told everything he knew to be true was a lie. But, yes, she needed to relax. Besides, an afternoon of festivities might be all she needed to put things into perspective. Plus, she was looking forward to seeing him again.

Tall and handsome with a sexy stubble, something she'd always found attractive, Alkazar had medium-length hair with natural waves and bright blue eyes. He looked similar to all the other Tsinians, yet there was something else. If only she could read him better. Some hurt, perhaps, that he hid away, past troubles. She wanted to understand him as he understood her. He was the only one who seemed to know how she felt.

The villagers spent the entire morning preparing for the princess's first meeting with her subjects. They were eager to meet Thya and rejoiced in her acceptance of who she was. There had been a rumour circulating the village that all was not well, only now it seemed further from the truth. The Tsinians wanted to celebrate the return of their princess and of the coming peace between the two lands. They believed the last of their troubles were behind them now Thya had returned.

Thya soaked in a warm, relaxing bath. The fragrance of lavender and peaches filled the air. But was it water, she wondered? Although it had the right colour and appearance, the consistency was too thick, and it was like bathing in cream. She didn't want the experience to end. Her spirit revived, and by the time Kezar came to dry her, Thya was singing a haunting melody that seemed to come from nowhere.

"You retain a remarkable voice, my lady. Could I inquire where you were acquainted with the melody?"

"I made it up."

Kezar stopped what she was doing, and it looked to Thya as though she wanted to say something. But then the Tsinian shook her head, smiled, and continued pampering and dressing her while talking non-stop about the festival and how everyone had spent the night preparing for her entertainment.

Thya was dressed in a white silk tunic with a train attached to the back. A thin gold braid hung around her waist. Single stone diamonds held the thin straps of the dress. Well, they looked like diamonds. The top of the tunic curved along her cleavage, retaining her modesty. She looked stunning, and all that was missing was a crown. Kezar brushed Thya's hair until it shone then braided the sides so they hung loose around her face.

Should it feel wrong to have someone dress her? No. She liked the pampering; it made her feel noble and ready to step into the role expected of her. She recalled Alkazar's words. 'Exist for the present.' And that was exactly what she was doing.

Kezar stood beside Thya as they both studied her reflection.

"You are cheering to the eyes, my lady."

"I wish I could say the same about you," said Thya. "You are a beautiful person… I mean, Tsinian. Why do you hide your beauty under drab clothes? And you should do something with your hair. It covers your stunning face."

Kezar blushed as Thya touched her face.

"Are you married yet? Married. You know, have a mate?"

Kezar looked down to the floor, embarrassed. "I am not yet at the… age for betrothal."

"I will make it my duty to find you a match." Thya laughed. "Now, as my attendant, I expect you to dress the part." She looked Kezar up and down. "Umm… yes. Put on the dress I wore yesterday. You are the same build as me, so it should be a perfect fit."

"Oh, I could not." Kezar gasped. "It would not be fitting."

"As your princess, I demand this from you." Thya smiled. "And do something with your hair. Pin it up or something. Well, come on, hurry up. Everyone will be waiting for us."

Kezar's ecstatic grin warmed Thya's heart.

It wasn't long before Kezar was ready, and, as Thya expected, she looked beautiful. It reminded Thya of a scene in My Fair Lady where the professor took Eliza Doolittle to a ball.

"I will have to be careful you don't outshine your princess," Thya joked.

"Oh, I could not do that. I would never. You are too exquisite, Thya. There is not one who could bear comparison to your loveliness."

"Steady on, girl. It's a figure of speech. Thank you for the flattery, even if it's a little overdone. I wouldn't have you looking any different. You look sensational and will have all the male Tsinians falling at your feet."

They both laughed. Thya took Kezar's hands and gazed at her.

"You are beautiful, Kezar, and you have a gentle nature. I am proud to have you as my friend. I know you think of me as your princess. Only, think of me also as Becky, a young woman – sorry, Tsinian – like yourself. Can you do this for me?" Thya twirled Kezar around to get a better look at her. "Your citizens will be proud of you."

"They are also your citizens," Kezar reminded her.

Thya forced a smile. She didn't want to think about that for the moment. She wanted to relax and enjoy the festivities. There would be plenty of time to worry about the future later.

A soft knock on the door disturbed her thoughts. The plump cook Thya had met the day before announced that Omad had arrived and was waiting for them in the attendance room.

"Kezar, will you see to Omad? Tell him I'll be there soon."

Kezar's brows knitted.

"Proceed to Omad. I will come," Thya repeated.

There was no way she would get used to their peculiar speech patterns.

Omad stared open-mouthed when Kezar walked into the room. "Kezar," blurted Omad, "you sight admirably."

She blushed and couldn't help but stare at Omad's

apparel. He wore a long, dark green velvet jacket, the collar of which displayed delicate gold embroidery. His trousers were velvet, too, and stopped just below the knee. They appraised one another and grinned. The door opened, and Thya strolled into the room, bringing with her an air of authority.

Omad took her hand and kissed it. "You are a striking sight. Your kinsmen will be overwhelmed by their princess."

"Thank you, Omad. You don't look too bad yourself."

"We ought to depart. Your subjects wait for your vision, only first…"

Omad reached into his pocket and pulled out a diamond-studded necklace. He passed it over to Kezar, who fastened it around Thya's neck.

Thya ran to the mirror to examine it. "It's amazing,"

She recalled an actress wearing something similar at the Oscars. The stones were big enough to be noticed, yet not oversized. The necklace was V-shaped, the point of which ended where her cleavage began. It gave her a sense of empowerment.

"This jewel was held by your mother," Omad told her. "Tis fitting that you be seen wearing it."

Thya caressed the stones. "My mother's," she whispered, blinking back the tears welling up in her eyes.

"The jewel has a place with you, my lady, and you

display it admirably. You look similar to your mother. She, too, was a remarkable Ganty, possessing both beauty and intellect."

Thya felt uncomfortable and embarrassed by all the compliments, though she could see the beauty they spoke of. "Thank you for your kind words. Let us leave."

Omad held his arm out for her to take, and Kezar opened the door ahead of them. The servants gathered outside the Recas bowed to her as she passed, and then followed behind. Thya noted they, too, had dressed for the occasion and that the festival seemed quite a big deal. She vowed not to let them down.

Thya watched Kezar's friends and acquaintances stare in awe at the girl's transformation and saw Kezar raise her head just as Omad puffed out his chest proudly. Thya grinned.

Wonderful fragrances and enchanting music engulfed Thya. The sound of a hundred orchestras filled the air. As they walked through the forest, cheers from the villagers echoed from their treetop dwellings. Silver streamers, confetti, and ribbons fell onto the gathering. Thya marvelled at the sight. Silver decorations adorned the green trees, making the city look even more magical.

The procession grew larger, and as her subjects joined, the laughter and love expanded. It warmed the centre of Thya's heart, and she felt honoured by the attention.

Omad led Thya to the Upess, which looked very similar to a sports arena. The villagers seated in the stands rose when she entered, their attention focused on their princess. Two Tsinians waved at her, and she recognised the joyful faces of Salco and Valcan. She returned their wave; however, her eyes searched for Alkazar. Only, she couldn't see him.

Omad directed her to the stalls reserved for royalty and motioned for her to sit. She felt a little apprehensive about it, as if doing so was a sign she had accepted her role to take the crown and rule Tsinia, which she had no intention of doing. Yes, she now knew her birth right and the truth of who she was, but that didn't mean she would submit to their orders.

It seemed stupid to stand when everybody was waiting for her to sit, so she did as Omad requested. Quiet murmurs filled the stadium.

To begin, Thya was introduced to the highly regarded Tsinians. There was no way she would remember their strange names, so she chose something about each person that stood out, hoping it would help her recall them.

Thya decided Valcan would be remembered for his bushy, chestnut beard.

"My lady, tis my delight to find you in good health," he said.

"Valcan, how can I ever repay you? You have a marvellous gift. Thank you for saving my life."

"I would replicate my performance a thousand turns over."

She giggled. "I hope that will not be necessary."

Nimas was next in line. Nimas the Nimble, she chuckled to herself, which, of course, was far from reality. The old Tsinian leant heavily on his staff. His eyes showed experience and knowledge. "I bestow praise to the Changlins for your secure return."

Thya didn't know how to reply but nodded her head anyway. He left, leaving her feeling dumbfounded. She felt as if she had just spoken to one of the oldest and wisest people she would ever meet.

When at last Thya spotted Alkazar, her heart pounded in her chest. She listened to the last few introductions, only her attention focused on Alkazar, who engaged in a heated conversation with a female. Though Thya hadn't met the redhead before, she took an immediate dislike to her, which wasn't in her character. The couple noticed the line before them had disappeared and made their way to Thya.

"My lady, I introduce Siren, my betrothed."

Thya's heart dropped into the pit of her stomach. She swallowed hard. "Alkazar, it's wonderful to see you again. Siren, it is a pleasure to meet you. Good luck to you both."

That was as pleasant as she was going to be. Even

though Siren had done nothing to cause Thya's dislike, Thya knew they would never become friends. She watched Alkazar leading Siren away and felt oddly saddened and alone.

"Kezar, will you ask Alkazar and Siren to join me? I wish the presence of their company."

Once everyone settled in their seats, bells rang out to announce the start of the festivities. The arena filled with graceful female dancers. Each wore a costume made of muslin and silk. Pastel shades of pink and green flowed before Thya. The display reminded her of butterflies. So elegant and smooth were the dancers, their arms and legs moved gracefully in a contemporary style of ballet. Thya, spellbound, watched, having never seen anything like it before. An expression of their language, Alkazar had informed her. Thya was fascinated by the spectacle and saddened when it ended. She applauded enthusiastically.

"The name is Faykar. Tis our nation's dance performed in your honour," Omad told her.

"Please, thank them for me. That was beautiful."

"Certainly."

"If you will allow me pardon, my lady, tis my turn to amuse," Alkazar announced.

Thya felt a little uncomfortable sitting beside Siren, so she struck up a conversation with Omad, only it was cut short when the bells rang out again.

Thya watched as a Tsinian walked over to a

gathered group, Alkazar being one of them, and held out a leather pouch. One by one, they reached inside then touched their lips with the tips of their fingers. The strange act caused Thya's curiosity to stir. She couldn't make out what was in the bag, and, as far as she could see, they pulled nothing out.

A Tsinian with ginger hair stepped forward.

"My lady, I am named Pertius, from the generation of Mundox. I am the tutor of our code."

His voice rang out loud and clear, as though he was speaking into a microphone. The volume astonished Thya. Somehow, they could amplify their voices.

Pertius continued. "You may have sighted or learnt since your arrival that some Tsinians possess unique powers or gifts, as we prefer to name them. Sadly, not all exhibit these. I presently require aid from Alkazar, our tutor of the arts."

Alkazar opened his mouth, and, as before, his voice projected around the arena. "My lady, tis my pleasure to provide an introduction to Athron, a Tsinian who is valued highly."

Athron stepped forward and bowed. Thya acknowledged him with a nod.

"Unfortunately," Alkazar continued, "Athron's talents are still unpredictable. He cannot at this moment display his gift to you. Nonetheless, by your leave, he will attempt to explain his specialty." Alkazar stepped back, and Athron bowed again.

"I bear honour by this encounter, my lady, as it was

my father who foresaw your reinstatement. I am allied to the generations of Zeniths. We are born with the gift of Sight, able to sight and foretell impending occurrences. As my good friend Alkazar had announced, I could progress into a trance at any duration. When this transpires, I am presented with images of expected events. While in this state, I inscribe the vision. Unfortunately, tis in form of a conundrum that only I can decipher. When I am released from this stupor, I do not recall the vision, yet I retain an understanding of the context. Tis then my duty to inform the council of my findings.

"Tis I who forewarned the council of the attack on Earth, and I dislike announcing to you that the Oracle was disregarded." There was a sudden rupture of murmuring in the crowd.

Alkazar stepped forward. "Athron, tis not the place!"

Once Athron's words sunk in, Thya realised the seriousness of his words and turned to Omad. "Does Athron speak the truth?"

"He does, my lady. It was a grave error, for which the council will always be regretful."

"Good, Athron," Thya called. "Omad, head of the council, has given me his word that never will an Oracle be ignored again. You will always be taken in earnest. Does this satisfy you?"

All eyes were upon the white-faced councillor. Omad rose. "I pledge by the grace of the Changlins that any reading you present will be judged accordingly."

Even though Athron wasn't convinced by Omad's assurance, he accepted graciously. "Tis all I require."

He bowed to Thya then glanced at Alkazar, whose face blazed with anger. He knew he would receive Alkazar's wrath for speaking out of turn.

"Good, Alkazar. Continue, please," Thya said.

Alkazar's anger cooled, his calm stature reappeared, and he introduced Thya to the others who possessed gifts.

Sparto, from the generation of Humal, possessed the gift of Illusor and could create illusions, which he did so magnificently and caused a cry of alarm as a fierce dragon appeared before them all.

"I also am aligned to the house of Humal," Siren informed her in a hushed whisper.

Next was Grenko from the generation of Bolarg, who, as Thya had already learnt, could grow nature. This she saw for herself when he presented her with a single rose that grew instantly from the ground, blooming while she held it in her hand.

Athania, a female from the generation of Ifreas, could control and communicate with animals. A large insect resembling a huge butterfly flew down and landed on Thya's knee. It made a sound like a trill, only sweeter. Thya gasped and her eyes open wide as it sang the melody she had hummed whilst bathing.

Lastly, Thya met Jenin, a female from the

generation of Devka, who had the ability to freeze objects. Jenin displayed her gift by freezing the rose Grenko had grown.

"The flower now retains eternal existence, as does the light that shines within you. Maintain it as a remembrance of your introduction to your loyal subjects."

From then on, Thya held the Tsinians in awe of their gifts and importance, yet she was also fearful of their power and strength.

After the completion of Alkazar's introductions, there was a brief interlude for refreshments before the lupa tournament began. Alkazar joined Thya in a glass of sweet wine made from the succulent berries of the forest. She felt warm and relaxed as she listened to Alkazar explain the rules of lupa.

The lupa, a laurel made of leaves and twigs, passed from one team member to another until it reached the end of the arena. Once there, the nearest player would throw the lupa over a pole, gaining their team a point. The team with the highest points were the winners. The other team would try and defend by catching the lupa in mid-air. There were only two rules. Firstly, the player who held the lupa was not allowed to move until it had left his hand. Secondly, the defending team couldn't take the lupa by force.

Thya didn't feel the need to share the news that they had a game in England almost identical to lupa. Alkazar explained the rules with such passion that

Thya could have listened to his voice for the rest of the day.

"We will sight upon a fervent game in honour of your presence," Omad said. "We amuse ourselves in recreation only. Despite this, the participants are eager to attain the reward and will compete in fierce competition."

"And what is the reward?" Alkazar inquired.

Omad coughed awkwardly. "With your allowance, my lady, I pledged your favour to the victorious team." He blushed.

Thya wasn't sure what that meant; although, from the look on Alkazar's face, she had a rough idea.

"My dear friend," Alkazar said, "I would recommend you converse with our lady before granting such a flirtatious reward."

Thya was still uncertain what she was supposed to give or do. Even so, she smiled and rested her hand on Alkazar's shoulder. "Relax, Alkazar. You have my permission, Omad. What better way to identify with my citizens?" She winked at Alkazar.

"Wonderful!" Omad cried.

Thya saw him breathe out in relief.

The teams entered the arena. One Tsinian from every team carried a coloured silk flag to represent their team. It was then Thya noticed an array of colours in the crowd. It seemed each villager had a preference. There were four teams: blue, red, silver, and gold. In turn, the teams paraded around the arena to cheers and jeers from the audience. They stopped briefly to show their respect to the princess.

Thya felt honoured and returned their bow with a smile and a slight nod of her head. She was astounded by the spectacle. She had never been a sports spectator, let alone a V.I.P. at an event.

A dull horn sounded the start of the tournament. It was fast-paced and ruthless, with players smashing into one another hoping to grasp the lupa. Oohs and aahs escaped from the engrossed audience. The atmosphere was electric, and Thya was soon caught up in the game. The first time a team scored a point, she stood and clapped enthusiastically, causing the scorer to blush and bow in response.

There was a short break before the final match. Thya was breathless from excitement and clapped hard for the winning team.

"Wow, that was amazing. I have never seen anything like it. You really do get swept away in it, do you not?"

Omad and Alkazar laughed.

Siren left to speak to a friend, and, soon after, Omad made his excuses to leave. "If you will absolve my departure, my lady, I speculate that my fellow Tsinians desire to converse."

Thya watched as Omad walked over to a group of Tsinians that were similarly clothed. They patted him on his back as if in congratulations.

She turned her attention back to Alkazar. She

smiled at him, and their eyes locked until Alkazar broke away.

"Who do you surmise will be victorious?" he asked.

"I'm sure the Silver Knights will win. They seem to be the stronger of the two. You are more familiar with the game, though. Who do you think will win my favour?"

Alkazar laughed. "Nay, my lady. I disagree with your outcome. The team coloured red will triumph, for they are swifter."

"Oh, I agree the Red Dragons have more speed. Call it woman's intuition, if you will, only I am certain the Silver Knights will win."

Alkazar threw back his head and laughed. "You possess strange expressions, Thya. Although if we ruled our land on intuition, as you name it, we would have lost our land to Darthorn long ago."

Thya bent her head as she thought about what he said and then shaking away the bad thought, she smiled and clapped her hands. "So, a bet then?" she cried. "What will you give me if my team wins?"

"You retain the whole of Tsinia at your feet. What could I possess that you would claim as your reward?"

Thya didn't reply.

Leaning in closer, he lowered his voice. "More to the point, my lady, what could you offer me?" His eyes bored into her soul. "Alas, regretfully, I will decline."

"Why so?"

His eyes shone as did his smile. "I do not gamble, for I am fearful of the amount I could lose."

He smiled again, only his eyes turned sad and his grin faded. "Pardon, my lady. Unfortunately, I am requested elsewhere. I hope you enjoy the remainder of the tournament. I look forward to concluding our conversation." He bowed and then left.

To Thya's annoyance, Siren met him. She took his arm and guided him to the other side of the arena, but not before glancing over her shoulder and giving Thya a triumphant look. Thya turned away when what she should have done was smile and wave back. Why give Siren the satisfaction of knowing how uncomfortable she was at seeing them together?

Thya couldn't concentrate on the final match. Even though she tried not to, she spent most of the game watching Siren and Alkazar. Her attention was finally awakened by the applause of the audience when a team scored a point. As it was now expected, she stood and clapped the scorer, only it was without emotion or enthusiasm.

Thya couldn't turn her focus away from the pair. Siren made it obvious that she lay claim to Alkazar, clinging to his arm and whispering in his ear. However, Alkazar's attention was fixed on the game. He hardly acknowledged Siren's flirting.

It seemed to Thya that the final game was never-ending when, at last, a gong rang out. The Silver Knights were victorious. It was her moment to shine.

Omad took her by the arm and led her to the heart of the arena where the players waited for their princess. Other esteemed Tsinians, including Alkazar, joined them. There was a hushed silence as the crowd awaited Thya's word. She knew what she wanted to say, just not how to phrase it. To annoy Siren and prove she did have a claim on Alkazar, she called to him. "Alkazar, a moment if you will?"

Alkazar looked embarrassed to be called for counsel in front of his peers, but he was soon by her side. She turned her back to the others and whispered to him. "I wish to invite the winners for refreshments at my new home, but I'm not sure how to ask them correctly."

Alkazar smiled.

"Firstly, princess, your home is named the Recas, and tis a great honour to be invited there. Few have seen the inside of our ruler's abode. This is well done. Secondly, as you are aware, we do not waste our duration with dates and times. So, bid them to attend you in one tril moon. What a tril moon is will be explained in due course. Tis not the correct place for conversing."

"Thanks, Alkazar. I knew I could count on you."

He bowed and returned to his position.

Thya spoke to each of the players, asking for their names and chatting about the game. The council watched as their princess joked and laughed with her subjects. The invitation to the Recas was received well. Applause filled the arena.

Once the presentation had ended, Thya was directed to a marquee where an array of food was on display. The feast lay across five long wooden tables. The villagers had outdone themselves. There were sweet breads, succulent meats, puddings, and even salad vegetables. Thya wanted to thank Grenko because she was sure he was responsible for growing the food. She searched for him and finally found him talking with Nimas and Athania. Only before Thya could approach, a ginger headed Tsinian blocked her path.

"Greetings, my lady."

"Hello, Pertius."

"I hope you are favouring our humble gathering and that the tournament was not too tedious for you."

"Not at all. It was very exciting; although, I have to admit it has been a long day, and I'm feeling tired. If you will excuse me, please."

Pertius paused before speaking again. "I understand tis not my station to inquire, only I am curious. I realise that not one has conversed with you thus far. I was wondering if you had received an awakening of your gift as of yet."

"As I am sure you know, I begin my first lesson with Alkazar tomorrow. However, if you're asking whether or not I can make things move, then I'm sorry to disappoint you. I was informed a Ganty is supposed to possess powers, only I do not. Or at least I don't think I do. You all have high expectations of me, and I don't want to let anyone down, but there you have it." She turned to leave, but Pertius grabbed her arm.

"All your kinsmen expect is for you to fulfil the prophecy and unite Tsinia and Senx in an alliance."

Thya turned to face him. "Senx?"

Pertius told Thya about Senx and of their ruler, Darthorn, leaving out no details. She listened, captivated by his passion of teaching her Tsinian history. When at last his mouth became dry from speech, he stopped.

Thya stared at him open-mouthed.

Finally, she spoke. "Why would you want to make an alliance with someone evil and dangerous? Are you not worried Darthorn will destroy everything good about Tsinia?"

Pertius proceeded to explain the Oracles.

Thya listened, though her eyes focused on the ugly, dark mountain that looked out of place beside the beauty of the forest. Though she couldn't see Darthorn's castle, she tried to visualise what it might look like.

"Okay," she said, "I understand. If the Oracles promised an alliance, and as you say they are never wrong, I have to take your word. What I don't understand is why I am here? How am I supposed to be your prophesied saviour?"

"Tis you who has been chosen to unite the alliance with Darthorn."

"You expect me to meet with this warlord and discuss peace with him? Are you mad? This has nothing to do with me. I know nothing of Tsinia. This is your fight, not mine. Send Omad. He is the highest ranking. It is he who should speak with Darthorn, not me." She calmed herself before continuing. "Still, I believe it's a bad idea. Is there no other alternative? Have you even thought about this?"

She took a step back as she watched Pertius's mouth open and close as if in shock.

"My lady, you misunderstand me. Has someone not disclosed why you were returned?"

"Certainly, I am to redeem you all," Thya said and flung out her arms dramatically.

Thya sensed the conversation was turning serious. It seems I'm going to find out why my life has been ruined.

"Tis the coming matrimony between yourself and Darthorn's son, Kovon, that will cement the alliance between the two lands."

Thya's face paled, and she couldn't move or find the words to speak.

"W-what?" Thya stuttered. "What did you say?"

"The wedlock between Kovon and yourself, tis agreed upon," Pertius answered, raising his eyebrows.

"It most certainly is not!"

Her raised voice stopped the music and laughter, and even Alkazar froze. All were witness to her rage.

"How dare you presume I would meet with Darthorn, let alone marry his son? Now you listen to me, and you listen well. You kidnapped me from my home, took me away from everything I hold dear, took my life away without my consent, and now expect me to marry the last person I would ever consider for a husband. I would rather die."

Lightning struck overhead. Thya turned to the crowd and found Alkazar.

"I renounce my title. I never asked for any of this, and I want naught. I want to go home, and I demand you return me." Tears flowed down her face. "I cannot aid you. This is not my fight. I'm sorry." Then she fled from the astonished crowd.

For one stunned moment, no one knew what to say or how to react. The murmurs began, and the council signalled Omad to go after her. Already, Alkazar was on her trail.

Thya ran into the forest, continuing until her strength could take her no farther. She collapsed and wept. The pursuers reached Thya together, and Omad was unsure what to say.

"M-my lady," he stammered.

"Go away. Leave me alone."

"Princess," Alkazar gently called.

Thya looked up at him, her eyes red and sore. "You knew! And you didn't tell me!"

"It was not my duty to tell you, nor was it my intention for you to be informed like this. It was wrong of Pertius to announce it. It was not the correct moment or place."

"All of you have been planning my wedding before I even arrived in this cursed land, have you not?"

"You are just, my lady," Omad answered. "I have not awareness on what or how much Pertius has disclosed to you, only tis written in the Oracles. Tis your duty to aid your kinsmen."

Alkazar tutted loudly. Thya turned and wiped her tears as she spoke to them both. "I understand this. However, do you not think I should have been consulted before you arranged the rest of my life? Do I not have a say? If I really am the future queen of Tsinia, what grants you the right to organise my future? Who gave you this authority?"

"There was not duration to linger," Omad explained. "The threat of war is ever greater, and your prophesied return seemed the key to our difficulties. We believe you will convey peace to our land."

"Why marriage?" she asked. "Why can't you create an alliance without my involvement, if you are certain this is all that's needed?"

"Darthorn would not agree to this. It was his condition," Omad answered.

"Oh, now I understand. Do you not understand

what he's doing?   Already he is ruling Tsinia, and you're allowing him to command you. He is accustomed to having everything his own way. Well, not anymore. I refuse to marry Kovon, and I'm not changing my mind. However, I will try to aid you, as you deem it's my duty to do so. Now, leave me alone. Return to the council and come up with another solution for peace, and I will attempt to do the same."

Thya turned away from them. Omad bowed and departed while Alkazar dropped to the ground beside her. He played with the wood chips before grabbing a handful of dirt and placing it in Thya's hand.

"This is Tsinia, whether you accept this or not. Tis your home, your land. You are part of it, and it is part of you. It has and always will be. Your kinsmen depend on you, Thya. We cannot fight Darthorn. We barely have enough power to resist him, and he is gaining strength. There is no alternative."

"I never wanted this," she cried. "I feel like I'm living a nightmare I can't wake from. It's getting darker, and I'm drifting deeper. I can't see the light anymore. I don't feel like myself, and that scares me."

"Your looks and personality are changing to that of a Ganty. Soon, your speech and soul will become Tsinian."

"I don't want to alter. I feel suffocated, choked by the pressure upon me." Unable to control her grief any longer, Thya broke down again.

Alkazar felt pity for her. He understood the

emotions she was experiencing and wanted to console her, tell her everything would be okay. Only he would not lie. A perilous destiny lay before her, and he could not change that. But if it were possible, he would try to ease the blow. With that thought in mind, he pulled her close.

There they sat, holding each other in silence. The villagers returned to their dwellings. Some crept past them; others avoided the couple so not to disturb their private moment. Thya and Alkazar were unaware of the villagers' presences and sat together for some time. It wasn't until Thya felt something brush against her leg that her tears ended.

"What is that?" she asked, startled.

Down by her leg sat a strange-looking animal. It was similar to an English squirrel, except for the two bulging eyes at the top of its head and a long, thin tail.

"Do not be frightened by him," Alkazar said. "'Tis named a portie. They live in the forest; although, 'tis unusual for them to approach so close. I think he is fond of you."

"Hello there," Thya whispered.

The portie seemed wary but edged closer. Finally, it allowed Thya to stroke it.

Alkazar gasped. "These are timid animals and yet it is not wary of you."

Thya laughed as she played with the strange animal.

"There are many beautiful and wonderful things in

Tsinia, so much I want to demonstrate if you would allow me. You ought to feel proud of your land."

Thya stifled a yawn.

"Come, your emotions have exhausted you. I will escort you to the Recas." Alkazar pulled Thya up.

The portie, sensing the fun was over, ran up the nearest tree.

"Do not fear, my lady, for I am certain you will lay sight upon him again. I deem you have created a friend forever."

His words upset Thya. "I do not intend to stay, Alkazar. Once I have done my part, I will return home. Whatever that part may be."

"If that is your desire, so be it. Only do not yell if I try to persuade you otherwise."

Thya smiled.

They travelled the rest of the way in silence. By the time they reached the Recas, the sky had turned pink and both moons shone brightly.

"Rest well, my lady. I desire upon you pleasant dreams."

"I doubt it," she mumbled as she walked inside.

She was in no mood for company and so dismissed Kezar and undressed herself. As soon as her head settled on the pillow, she fell asleep, though her dreams were far from pleasant.

A tall, powerful man with jet-black hair haunted her. His voice carried a cruel tone, and she dreamt of winged horses and a cavern containing a black oval crystal. The voice was commanding, and it disturbed her. She awoke several times in a cold sweat. She forced her thoughts to envision the dream of her parents. They calmed her, and she slept peacefully.

Thya's Sessions

THYA WOKE TO A BREAKFAST OF JUICY forest fruits. Already, her head pained, and her limbs felt tired and sore. She wanted to lie in bed all day, only Kezar was having none of that.

"What glorious light," Kezar sang. "Come see, my lady. Even the trees are greener than usual. Tis a sign that all will be well. Come, you have an important engagement. I ought to ready you to receive Alkazar."

The mention of his name rose Thya's spirits. She thought it a good enough reason to get out of bed too.

Kezar dressed her in a red silk wrap dress, simple in design yet stunning to behold. Placing a large red wildflower, which she had picked earlier, in Thya's hair, she stood back to admire her work.

"There, I am satisfied," Kezar announced.

They heard a loud knock on the door.

"Already!" Thya exclaimed. "You don't waste any time, do you? Okay, show him to the attendance room. I will be there soon."

Kezar greeted Alkazar at the door. "Our lady will receive you shortly. Enter, Alkazar."

"You are well, Kezar?"

"Admirably. Tis an honour to serve our lady. She possesses a strange, yet wonderful, personality."

"I agree."

"Though I fear her heart is heavy."

Alkazar could not question Kezar further as Thya entered the room.

"I almost forgot about my lesson. Do you mind if we do this some other time? I am not feeling well. My head is killing me."

"Kezar, leave us," Alkazar instructed.

She turned to Thya for permission.

"It is fine, go," Thya told her.

Thya waited until Kezar left, then she poured some wine. Alkazar felt the need to speak.

"What you learnt ought not to have been conversed in that manner. The moment was not right."

"No, it was not," she snapped. "I should have been told from the start instead of being deceived. I refuse to marry anyone I do not love. No one will force me to, no matter the consequences. As I have said, I have a headache and do not wish to discuss this."

"I understand, Thya. Truly I do."

"How could you?"

"We Tsinians are betrothed since the coming of age. Are you familiar with when this is?"

"About sixteen human years?"

"Correct. Since this age, we are spoken for. I presume you name it as such. I do not love Siren, so I understand."

"Oh, I see." The unexpected news cheered Thya. "What happens if you fall in love with someone else – your soul mate? Someone other than your betrothed. What then?"

"The code forbids it."

"The code? What is this? A set of rules you have to follow?" She laughed.

Alkazar frowned, unhappy with her mockery.

"Who has the authority to modify the code when it is outdated? You ought to be allowed to love who you want, not be dictated to be with someone you don't love."

"'Tis not my place to discuss the code. Tis Pertius's task. I believe you are to have a session with him later. Remarking of which, I am present to tutor you … or have you forgotten?"

"Well, that was a subtle alteration of subject." She ignored Alkazar's puzzled expression. "I have not finished my conversation yet."

Thya sensed her questions were making him uncomfortable, only she was enjoying herself too much to stop. "Siren is very attractive. I cannot understand how falling in love with her can be such a trying task, especially for a man like – sorry, a Tsinian – like yourself."

"I am a man, my lady, in every sense of the word."

There was something dangerous gleaming in his eyes, urging Thya to push harder. "So, declare to me, Alkazar. Why could you not love Siren?"

"I will unite with her as tis my duty. Despite this, I will never love her. She does not contain enough spirit."

Thya laughed at this. "So, you want spice in your life?" she teased.

"I desire a Tsinian who can support herself and not hide behind her husband's shadow. One that exhibits brains as well as beauty."

His hypnotic eyes pierced her soul. It was too much for Thya to cope with. "Just because you will wed out of duty, do not expect me to do the same," she told him.

An awkward silence followed, then came a welcome knock. As if summoned by magic, Kezar appeared and waited for instruction.

"Bring your mistress a glass of tamin juice," Alkazar ordered. "I fear she has drunk much wine."

"Nonsense," Thya retorted. "This is my first glass."

Kezar left at his request.

"Tis not wise to drink alcohol when we are in

session," he explained. "Tamin juice stimulates the brain."

"Well, I hope it tastes nice," Thya teased. She sighed. "If I must go through with this ridiculous charade, then at least reveal something about this so-called power I am supposed to possess."

"Do you doubt it, princess?"

"Of course I do. If it were true, why have I not sighted anything by now? You're wrong about me, and the sooner you realise this, the better for us all."

"We will soon see." He smiled. "And in answer to your inquiry, Thya, our powers, or gifts as I prefer to name them, are unobtainable in your era."

"So, if, let's state, I have this gift, I will be powerless when I return home?"

"Tis correct. This is why you have not seen any sign of it before."

"How far do your gifts reach? Tsinia? Senx?"

Alkazar thought for a moment. "Your planet is named Earth, and your land is England. Enumac is the name we present to our world, though we do not consider Enumac a planet. We are in another dimension from you. Enumac is the name of the lands as far as we can reach. Each land is occupied and labelled by a different race. We Tsinians and, unfortunately, the Senxs belong to a race called Bora. I am certain there is more of our kind beyond the Outlands, only that is yet to be explored." Resting his hand on his hip, he glared at Thya. "I refuse to remark another word on this. Tis Pertius's task."

Thya had a lot to think about. Even so, her head was hurting too much, and she couldn't take it all in.

Kezar arrived with refreshments.

The tamin juice was sweet and cold, like thick sorbet.

"Umm, this is delicious. What is it?" she asked.

"A concoction of mine. A mixture of forest berries and other ingredients, which I will not disclose. I require all my students to drink it prior to a session. Kezar, leave us."

Alkazar waited until the door closed before continuing. "I am aware of your discomfort. I can see by the colour of your eyes your head pains you. Come, sit beside me. I have a remedy that will cure your ills."

Thya did as he asked and waited for his next instruction.

"Tilt your head back, not too far. That is sufficient. Close your eyes and breathe deeply. Now relax."

Thya's head rested upon Alkazar's chest. His fingers pressed on either side of her temples, massaging gently. Warmth emitted from his fingertips, and already the pain was subsiding.

"That feels so good." She sighed. "You have healing hands."

"Nay, Thya. That is Valcan's gift. Part of your training is learning to relax, and, fortunately, I have experience in that activity. You are tense. I am aware of your stress. What you have discovered and sighted may seem unreal to you. I am responsive to your ordeal. Regardless, in order to get through this, you are to control your emotions."

"Umm," she replied, hardly listening to what he was saying.

His hands lowered down to the top of her neck. His massage continued, lower still, down to her shoulders. The rubbing and pressing deepened, becoming more intense.

Thya was feeling good. So relaxed she thought she might fall asleep.

Alkazar slipped the silk straps off her shoulder. His fingertips caressed her skin, causing ripples of delight to run through her body.

How far is he willing to go? I'm aroused by his gentle touch. I want more. His hands wandered further down the front of Thya's neck, as if guided by her will. Then stopped just as he approached her breasts.

"Umm… don't stop," she breathed.

As if her words sent a shock through his hands, he removed them. She opened her eyes wide.

"I fear you are too relaxed," he told her. "I cannot have my students falling asleep on me."

There was an awkward silence. Thya was finding it difficult to compose herself.

"You are fit to begin," he announced.

Sitting up, she tried to concentrate. He walked around to face her. She tried her hardest to give him her fullest attention, but her mind kept drifting back to the feel of his touch. She imagined him leaning down to kiss her mouth.

"Do you understand?" Alkazar repeated, a little louder.

Thya quickly became alert. "I am sorry. What did you remark?"

"Thya, if you will not concentrate, you are wasting our session."

"I am sorry, Alkazar. I will try harder." She smiled.

He huffed and stared at her. She wondered just what he was thinking when he announced. "Perhaps some fresh air will awaken you. We will continue outside on the balcony." His hand pointed to the glass doors.

The cool air refreshed her, and she was soon wide awake. Alkazar brought a seat out from the room and asked her to sit.

"As I was trying to convey to you, the gift you possess is named Flite. You have the ability to move objects with your mind. All Ganties possess this gift, and tis my pleasured duty to tutor you in the employment of your talents. To move an object, you are required to reach the Owto, a place between conscious and unconscious."

"Sort of like a trance?"

"Similar to a hypnotic state," he answered. "You

ought to be aware of things around you and pay attention to conversations, yet you need to be able to detach yourself from reality so you can concentrate on what you desire. It is rather like splitting your mind in two."

"Sounds hard."

Alkazar laughed. "It can be. It depends on how receptive you are. Let us attempt?"

"Sure, what have I got to lose?"

"Start by relaxing your body. Close your mind and relax in the chair; feel your body loosen. When you think you cannot go further, push your body deeper." He saw Thya push herself back into the chair. "Employ only your thoughts. Do not employ your physical being." Thya relaxed once again. "Better. Melt into the chair. Become one with the wood. Breathe deeply. Inhale through your nose, and exhale through your mouth. That's it. Keep breathing deeper. Good. You ought to feel as though you are drifting." Thya nodded slightly. "I require you to imagine space as you understand it to be: be darkness all around you, apart from the stars and planets surrounding your view. You are alone, moving through space, drifting. Detach your mind and focus on the darkness – on the silence. Concentrate, Thya." He paused for a moment. "The stars and planets are fading, and there is naught but utter darkness. Still, you move through the blackness."

Thya was coming to the crucial part. Alkazar

moved closer. He lifted one of her eyelids and saw her pupil was stationary and her breathing steady. Both were good signs. Just for a moment, he felt the urge to lean in and kiss her but pushed the thought aside. He scolded himself. He was supposed to be teaching her how to concentrate yet struggled with his own.

"Continue moving through the darkness," he continued. "Soon, you will come to a suspended door. Tis grey in colour. When you arrive, grasp the handle until I instruct you to –"

"I sight the door," Thya called out.

"Continue to grasp the handle. When I command you to unlock it, I want you to open your eyes. Are you prepared?"

"I am," she answered.

"Unlock."

Thya opened her eyes, blinked twice, and then smiled at him. "So, how did I do?"

Alkazar wasn't surprised she did not reach the Owto; they rarely did on their first arrival at the door. However, he was surprised by how far she had gone.

"Very good. Only you have to concentrate harder. Relate to me, what colour was the door?"

"Umm… a light grey with black marks."

"You have done well. We will discontinue for the moment. You ought to rest, as you will be tired. I will request that Pertius does not announce himself."

"Thanks, Alkazar. I do not think I can take any of his talk of doom and gloom."

Alkazar laughed. "Pertius has much to instruct you about your legacy, the past, and of your future. It does not have to be as doomed as you remark. I am confident that once you have conversed you will find a sudden interest to learn all."

"If you state so," she replied casually.

"Rest if you can. However, I declare that after our session your mind will be wandering." He turned to leave, pausing at the door. "Understand this, Thya. If you ever require me as a friend or as a tutor, you have only to summon and I will attend you. This I vow. For the present, farewell." He bowed then left.

Alkazar was correct in his statement. No matter how she tried to relax, she found it impossible. She could not sleep, and, when sitting, her mind would not concentrate. It was as if she was awake for the first time in her life. Even though she could not focus on one thought, her mind was clearer than ever before. Thya felt the need for fresh air and exploration of her new awakenings.

Alkazar eventually found Pertius in the dwelling of Nimas. Their speech halted when they noticed him standing by the door.

"Enter, Alkazar. Welcome friend," Nimas greeted. "How does our princess fare?"

"Praise to the Changlins," Alkazar answered before entering.

Nimas motioned for Alkazar to sit beside him, then poured him some wine.

Pertius cleared his throat. "I have been conversing with Nimas, planning my session for our lady. There is much to educate and little duration."

"I agree, Pertius, which is why I am present. I understand the requirement for our lady's tutor, only she does not fare well."

"How so?" Pertius asked, a note of concern etched in his voice.

"A slight ache." Alkazar waved his hand dismissively. "'Tis not my concern, though. If you would reflect on her situation for a moment – what she has learnt, what has been revealed to her – I compel you to sympathize with the emotions our lady is experiencing. I am without doubt that if pushed any further… well, friends, you understand my meaning."

Pertius attempted to speak. "I recognise this only – "

"Also, I will declare, it was not wise to converse with her on a subject she knew naught about and at a period unsuitable."

"I am of the same opinion," Nimas agreed.

"I was in error," Pertius admitted. "I was in haste

to encounter and educate our lady. I did not consider the consequences. You apprehend the urgency? We cannot delay the introduction."

"With certainty," Alkazar replied. "Only, would a short delay cost so much? I assure you, Pertius, she is an apt pupil and will gain an understanding quickly. It should have taken three or four sessions until a student sights the door and yet Thya came upon it on her first lesson. "

Pertius bent his head and then stiffened. "That is surprising news. Nevertheless, am I to understand that you had session with her yet refuse my own? I strongly disagree with this." He looked to Nimas for support.

Nimas frowned. "Surely you overreact, Alkazar. If she is sound enough to partake in session with you, how can she not attend session with Pertius? Nay, I have sighted her myself, and she appears in control. Although, I agree that with what has been displayed to her, I, myself, would feel astray and confused. Alas, I concur with Pertius; she urgently requires tutor in both the arts and the code. What duration is Darthorn willing to linger? Already I sense his impatience. To stall further could be peril, and Omad will not permit the encounter until our lady is skilled in both our crafts. Nay, a delay could be serious. Send for Valcan. If his opinion states a postponement, then so be it. Is this agreed?"

"Agreed," they chorused.

Pertius left in search of Valcan.

Nimas studied Alkazar. "You desire to converse with me on a matter of some importance."

Alkazar forced a small smile. "As always, naught can pass you, wise one. I am correct in my statement; our lady requires rest. I believe Valcan will agree with me. Despite this, I did escalate a small touch."

"A small touch." Nimas smiled. "So, declare to me. Did your session progress well?"

"I am amazed by her development, how quickly our lady is modifying to her surroundings. Her appearance and speech are maturing at an astounding rate. There is something strange, yet wonderful about her. I cannot comprehend exactly what it is."

"A glow?" Nimas queried.

"You recognize it also?"

"Nay, I sight not light. Nonetheless, I feel, as do all who view her, a power or force surrounding her. I am confident that once you educate the princess in her gifts, you will find the answers you seek."

"I, too, am assured of this. Never has a student progressed so far in one session. The next will find our lady in the Owto. This I am convinced of."

Nimas's eyes lit up. "Wonderful tidings and so rapidly. You did not exaggerate, Alkazar."

"I possess an understanding, yet I do not comprehend why. I believe Thya to be more powerful than we first thought. I even speculated she would reach the Owto on her first attempt, which, of course, is unexpected. Somehow, deep in her soul, she carries a will stronger than her own. I confess I have never encountered a Tsinian surrounded by so much energy. I am of the opinion that she is a very unique Ganty."

Alkazar did not mention it was the meaning of this strange energy that scared him.

"I do not disagree with your thoughts, Alkazar. We all sense the power, and you, my friend, retain the task of unleashing that hidden force. Only, I will express my view on a worry I hold."

Alkazar leaned in closer.

"I am not blind; neither are those who surround you. The princess favours you; this is obvious. She calls upon your counsel above all others. I am gratified she places enough trust in you to confide. Despite this, others have conversed with me their concern. Do not allow forgetfulness of your loyalties. Thya is a princess and the rightful heir of Tsinia, and you, Alkazar, are betrothed to Siren. Become a confidante and attend her counsel. Only I forewarn you: do not tread further, for tis forbidden."

Alkazar looked shamefully to the floor. Were his feelings so obvious? He had embarrassed himself and shamed Siren's name. He would right the wrong before word spread further.

"If I have faltered, Nimas, tis because of her beauty. Our lady possesses a lure to all. To exhibit my honour, I will converse with Siren's generation and prepare for our union." Although he spoke with confidence, his insides churned.

"Tis well, Alkazar. The princess does not require an added distraction to an already difficult fate. Praise to the Changlins."

Alkazar bowed then left. He needed to go over the conversation and let the words sink in. He had landed himself in a dangerous situation.

Back on Senx, Darthorn received the news of Thya's unfortunate recovery.

"So, she survived," Darthorn said. "It grieves me much, though why was I informed of her ill health by Omad when Jakar observed her walking unaided around her precious land? Why the delay, I wonder?"

"Why, indeed," Kovon answered.

The messenger looked startled by Kovon's sudden appearance. Only Darthorn sensed his son's entrance. The messenger knew his exit and left quickly, leaving father and son alone.

"Does it not trouble you, Father? Tis but Thya's word for the delay. The peasants are feeble and eager for peace and for the alliance; they long to sign without haste. So, why do you suppose Thya has demanded a postponement?"

Darthorn turned to face his son.

Kovon continued. "I declare that she has refused

to encounter with you. Indeed, I am convinced that she has not accepted the title freely, if at all."

"Indeed," agreed Darthorn. "How so?"

"I sense concern amongst the villagers, and Jakar spoke of a disagreement at their festival. I imagine you will discover me just."

Darthorn called for a messenger.

"Dispatch word to Tsinia," he instructed. "Darthorn agrees that the delay is just, and he desires their princess a speedy recovery. He requests to encounter with her in five tril moons."

The messenger departed.

"A delay could cost us dearly," Kovon protested.

"Nay allow her space. Suppose she refuses to aid her kinsmen. I become victorious and will at last rule Tsinia. If she agrees to the union, then you will encounter your betrothed. Either method is to my advantage." He smiled, content.

"I disagree."

"'Tis my command," Darthorn growled. "Dare you quarrel with the lord of Senx? Detain your anger and wrath for when you receive your title. Until then, remain silent."

Kovon turned and stormed out of the hall.

Pertius was on his way to the Tora in search of Valcan when he glimpsed Thya as she walked among the trees. He judged that she appeared well and decided to follow her.

Knowing she wouldn't be able to leave the Recas without an escort, Thya had climbed over the balcony and sneaked into the forest. Even so, the walk didn't refresh her as she had hoped. She had more privacy alone in her room than she did in the open. Thya could feel eyes following her, and every now and then, a call would rain down upon her.

"Praise to the Changlins" or "Greetings, my lady."

Thya changed her path many times but still heard the cries from above. How was she to get peace when she had the constant annoyance of being watched? Out of the corner of her eye, she saw a shadow; someone was following her. Not Alkazar, though. She turned around and faced the hidden watcher.

"Whoever you are, I demand you show yourself."

No sooner were her words spoken than the sullen face of Pertius came into view.

"Pardon the intrusion, my lady. I was in search of you. Alkazar related your ills, and I was concerned. If you permit me to remark, tis not wise to travel unaccompanied. Darthorn has many eyes."

The mere mention of his name sent shivers down her spine.

"I thank you for your concern. Nevertheless, is it

not rude to sneak around like the enemy? You gave me quite a fright."

"Pardon my intrusion. I will not detain you further." He turned to leave.

"Nay, wait! Stay a while and walk with me. I have questions that need answers, and you, I am told, are the one to satisfy them."

"As you command."

So, their session began, and while they wandered through the forest, Pertius talked of the generations of Ganties and how her late mother and father ruled the land and their gentle character. He even spoke of the many times Darthorn had tried to attack Tsinia and how they counteracted his useless attempt. Thya laughed at Pertius's expression, delighted that her Kinsmen were gifted enough to outplay the warlord of Senx. Thya listened intently, eager to learn all he divulged. Early evening came and still they talked. Even though Thya felt a chill, she wouldn't allow Pertius to stop until all the questions that were in her head were answered.

"My lady, it has grown late, and we have conversed much. I have taken too long in your company. Kezar will be in search of you if we do not produce an appearance."

Thya laughed. "I don't think anyone has missed me, for there have been eyes following us everywhere we have walked. I am sure all are aware of our location."

It was Pertius's turn to laugh. "I do not doubt this."

Thya continued to ask him questions and listened to him with rapt attention.

"Declare to me, Pertius. If I wanted to get away from these prying eyes" – she signalled to the tree dwellings – "where would I go?"

"To be unsighted, you would have to journey to the Outlands, some distance from our borders and absent from the protection of the Changlins. Alas, tis forbidden to depart the forest."

"The code forbids you to leave Tsinia?"

"Nay, not the code. We are unacknowledged in the Outlands, and those who have dared to venture have not returned. For what reason could we possess the desire to depart? Our dwellings and all we require is provided by the grace of the Changlins."

"Are you not curious to know what is out there? Would you not like to explore beyond your borders? I believe I would."

"I am informed about terrible evils, monsters, and strange creatures. I choose to exist secure and contented."

Thya wanted to discuss it further, but because it was so late, she gave in.

"I suppose you are correct. Well, I confess, I'm lost. You'll have to escort me back to the Recas."

"Tis my honour." He held out his arm for her.

"I thank you for a pleasant afternoon, Pertius. You

are a good tutor, and I look forward to our next encounter."

"As do I, Thya. I will converse with Omad and surely be scorned for keeping long in your company, though my tour with you was worth any tongue lashing."

Thya chuckled.

"If he gives you any bother, tell him I kidnapped you."

Pertius looked puzzled.

"Stole you," she added, wondering if she would ever get used to their vocabulary.

"Very well. Rest easy, my lady."

Pertius watched Thya enter the Recas before leaving.

Even though she felt content as she snuggled under the silk sheets, she did not wake with the same emotion. Her sleep was again disturbed by horrid dreams of a dark voice instructing her. There were other voices, too, the ones she had heard in the Plecky, soothing voices that dulled the sharpness of the evil tone.

A new Tsinian day began, but the brightness could not cheer the fear instilled into Thya's bones. She ate breakfast alone, preferring solitude to Kezar's company. Thya sensed an atmosphere, tenseness, as though the land was waiting for something. The burden weighed heavily, and she could barely walk. A decision was needed, yet all she wanted to do was curl up and die.

She was given plenty of time to consider the questions racing through her mind as Alkazar arrived for their session long after lunch, looking even more handsome than before.

Senx

THYA TRIED TO MAKE POLITE conversation, only her heart wasn't in it. She spoke of her session with Pertius, but her words were negative, or so Alkazar thought. She seemed restless, certainly not in the correct frame of mind to begin the session. It pained him to see her suffer, so he chose to liven her spirits as her smile and laughter lightened his heart.

"Come," he said. "We will take session among the trees."

They left the Recas and took the path that led to the Upess. There, Alkazar found a suitable spot under a shaded tree, which surprisingly wasn't inhabited. He laid a cloth on the ground and motioned for Thya to sit. While Alkazar poured the tamin juice, Thya eyed the black mountain.

Alkazar followed her gaze. "I can do naught to remedy your view. We Tsinians are forced to exist with that monstrosity in sight, a reminder that Darthorn is forever looking down upon us. What I would give for the gift of colouration. What do you surmise, my lady? Is pink a warm enough shade?"

Thya laughed, only it soon faded to silence. She sipped the juice, deep in thought. Alkazar knew the liquid calmed her; although, he sensed a shadow shroud her.

Alkazar took hold of her hand. "Declare your fears, for I believe you retain many."

She looked into his concerned eyes. "Though I still do not want to venture into Senx, and I refuse to unite with anyone so vile, I understand that tis my duty to do so. I predict that I will encounter with Darthorn as is expected of me. I am chosen, yet still I am unaware why. What is my destiny? What is my purpose? Tis such a weight, Alkazar. A responsibility I did not invite. Back home, I lived an ordinary existence. I was not special, and nobody depended on me. I was happy."

"I can only envisage how heavy your burden is, princess. You ought to be fearful, and not one will judge you for that. Tis good you are unnerved."

"How, Alkazar? Why is it good I'm scared? What if it does not proceed as tis expected? What if I fail you? You all demand so much of me, I doubt I can deliver. I deem myself selfish that I am more frightened for myself than for my kinsmen. I cannot anticipate what will occur in Senx. I fear for my being. Already, he has completed one attempt. I am convinced this is what he has planned. So, enlighten me, please. What is good about being scared?"

Alkazar regarded Thya. "You will recognise and be prepared for conflict. If you journey to Senx carrying arrogance and bravery, then I guarantee you will throw away any hope of an alliance. Nevertheless, if you are wary and maintain your senses to be sharp and alert, expecting trouble, then I believe you will succeed in your quest and will evolve into a stronger Tsinian. Come. Let us not dwell on what will be. The moment will arrive soon enough. You are not yet ready to encounter Darthorn, and Omad would not permit you to partake in such a meet until you are. I, too, will not permit this unless I deem you fit and able. Come, on to our session."

Thya was not satisfied. "What am I to expect?"

Alkazar sighed before turning to her.

"What can I declare to you to deliver you peace?"

"Converse with me about the attack on Tsinia, when the Ganties were slain."

Alkazar stared hard at her. She hoped he would talk about the tragedy. She needed to know.

"Darthorn employed the power of the Darkeye and cast a deadly mist to choke us all. Despite this, the danger was prophesied in an Oracle, and a fellow Tsinian named Athania was prepared and alert.

Athania retains the gift of Mynd, the ability to control animals. She commanded the birds of the forest to soar into the sky. They were unaffected by the poison, and with the flapping of many wings, the mist dispersed. In outrage, Darthorn unleashed a great army upon us led by Kovon."

Alkazar examined Thya's expression. It was unreadable, so he continued. "Voltim, who possesses the gift of Sonica, alerted us to their arrival, giving your parents adequate warning to send you away. Regretfully, they remained. The opening of the orb is situated on the outskirts of our borders, and our rulers ventured unprotected. I did not realise their intent. Many were engaged in the defence of our city. If we had recognised what would occur..." He stopped and bowed his head with regret.

"Who killed your king and queen?" Thya asked.

Alkazar lifted his head and sighed.

"'Tis claimed the hand of Kovon slew our rulers, although there was none to witness this. Thya, I beg of you, do not journey to Senx with vengeance in your heart and mind."

"I cannot grieve as I am unfamiliar with my parents. I was sixteen when I was informed of my adoption. It came as a shock and took a lot of time before I accepted the situation. Throughout this, not once did I consider searching for my natural parents. As far as I am concerned, I still have a loving mother and father on Earth."

Alkazar wasn't convinced Thya could throw aside her emotions so easily, even if she spoke without a care. He sensed her confusion between anguish and sorrow.

"If Kovon slayed the Ganties and I was one birthday old, that would make Kovon at least double my age."

"It would be so if Tsinian years were identical to Earth years, though he is older by some. I insist that we commence our session. I do not desire to face the wrath of Pertius. Suppose we venture into his strict schedule?"

"Okay, I get the message." Thya laughed. "I am prepared when you are."

Once Thya relaxed, Alkazar brought her to the Owto. This time, when she opened the suspended door, her eyes held a glazed look about them. She stared ahead for some time. Finally, she blinked.

"Very good," Alkazar announced. "What colour was the door?"

"Dark grey. Why do you always inquire about the colour?"

"The darker the shade, the closer you are to entering the Owto. You are very receptive, Thya. I believe you will presently be moving trees."

Once again, they reached the Owto. Only this time, he instructed her to concentrate on the glass of tamin juice when she opened her eyes, then demand it travel towards her. The exercise resulted in Thya tipping the glass and soaking the cloth they were sitting on, ending with them both collapsing in laughter.

"Excellent," Alkazar said through his giggles.

Thya's session with Pertius was also productive. They spoke of the language difference between her manner of speech and the Tsinian way.

She questioned Pertius on Tsinian night and day, hour and minutes.

"Time is not relevant to us," Pertius told her. "We proceed through our existence absent of plans and dates, except those which concern you, my lady." After a pause, he added, "We decipher the duration of a day, I believe you name it, by the appearance of our sky. For instance, observe if you will. How adjacent do you believe us to be to a tril moon?"

"A tril moon. What is this?"

"'Tis the name we describe for the alteration of the sky. Our two moons grow brighter, and the sky modifies into a pink shade. 'Tis named a tril moon."

"I have seen this tril moon. It was beautiful. We retain a similarity in my world. It's called a sunset."

Pertius looked interested. "I am unfamiliar with your world. Perhaps I ought to converse some with Alkazar. I could do well to gain an understanding of your existence. So, to my inquiry," he reminded her.

"Well, I had just retired when last I saw the wonderful sight you remark of. In my world, we call this night, and as I have spent many hours with both you and Alkazar, I guess that very soon we will see a tril moon."

"'Tis accurate." He smiled.

They ended their session and made their way back to the Recas. Through their travels, they came upon Valcan.

"Greetings, my lady. Pertius, how goes it with you?" Valcan inquired.

"Our lady is progressing well. She is a demanding student," Pertius told him.

"Very good. However, I deem your sessions are far too lengthy. You require rest, my lady. Tis not long ago you were unwell. A Bora can only endure a certain amount of information at one period. Rest, understood?"

"I do, Valcan," she replied meekly.

He nodded to them both then continued on his way.

"Valcan is just in his statement, Thya. You have absorbed much in the short duration you have been among us. You are required to relax, break from your sessions, and allow the information you have acquired to become understandable."

"I assure you, Pertius, if it becomes too much for me you will be the first to be informed. You fail to remember that I existed and was brought up in another land. My mind soaks up knowledge. Though, if tis permitted, I would like to take some time to explore Tsinia."

"An excellent notion. I will converse with Omad and Alkazar. I am confident they will permit this. You have learnt a great deal, more than we anticipated. I am informed that already you have reached the Owto. This is unique, yet very fitting. A break will not be of issue. If I could, I would visit upon you thereafter, in the event you have queries to put to me."

By the time they had reached the Recas, Thya had already planned out her day. She said goodbye to Pertius and hurried into the building.

Kezar and two kitchen attendants were busy preparing dinner when Thya burst in on them, and they looked up in surprise.

"Kezar, you and I will journey through Tsinia tomorrow. I mean, the next day. Oh, you understand my meaning, do you not?" she asked, frustrated. "I have the day off tomorrow, and we will walk and eat among the trees. What is your name?" Thya pointed to the plump cook.

"Rosina, my lady," she answered with a curtsy.

"Well, Rosina, I would like you to prepare a delicious lunch, one we can take with us. Thank you. I retire. Good night to you all." She bounded out of the kitchen, leaving them startled.

Thya and Kezar had a glorious time together. They walked for miles through the beautiful land. Although tree dwellings surrounded them, the land split into two, and Thya was stunned by the magnificent waterfalls and lakes within Tsinia's borders.

"Tis paradise," Thya declared.

They lunched beside crystal waters and luscious green hills.

"It's perfect. So calm and peaceful," Thya said.

Just then, a yell rang out, followed by echoed shouting.

Thya giggled. "Well, it was."

Three Tsinians ran out of the bushes, almost falling on them. "Pardon, my lady," one said breathlessly, embarrassed by the situation.

Thya bowed her head, and they took off again. Once alone, Thya and Kezar burst out laughing.

On their return, Kezar pointed out important tree dwellings, and introduced Thya to strange creatures and animals, and she was surprised to learn Thya was already acquainted with a Portie. She was amazed at how well the animal responded to her.

Thya bonded well with Kezar. She could open up to her as though she was the sister Thya had never had. They talked frankly about their hopes and fears. Thya listened to Kezar's tales of her adventures and of important events that had happened in Tsinia. Thya compared Kezar's life to her own and was surprised to discover she felt envious. Could she consider settling in Tsinia, having experienced such a different upbringing? For now, she was willing to enjoy her new surroundings and treasure her friendship, one they decided would last a lifetime.

The following days saw Thya studying hard in both the code and the use of her power of Flite, which she was mastering well. She was still unresolved in her decision and wished that every new light would bring a solution to the ever-growing crisis. Little did Thya know that her time was running out.

Several tril moons had passed when Omad received word from Senx. Darthorn demanded an encounter with Thya and would wait no longer. An emergency council was held.

"We have conversed among ourselves, Omad, and as the elected head of the council, tis your accountability to ensure our lady encounters with Darthorn. Tis our instruction, and if you fail, tis agreed that you will suffer the consequences," Tasark told him.

Omad was sorry he had ever accepted the position. Since becoming the head, he had not known restful sleep. Too much was demanded of him and far higher was the grave responsibility he was expected to bear. Now, it had come to this. He questioned what he should do, but only he knew the answer. Somehow, he had to persuade Thya to reconsider; it seemed now that his own future was in jeopardy.

Omad found Thya lunching with Kezar underneath the shade of a tree, close to the Upess.

"My lady pardon the intrusion. Tis pressing I converse with you. Kezar, you will depart."

"Very well. Only remain close at hand," Thya told Kezar.

Kezar left, walked a short distance, and sat on the ground waiting for Thya's call.

"What is the urgency, Omad? You look pale with fear. Please, sit. Inform me freely."

Omad seated himself upon the ground cross-legged. "You recognise our plight and realise your fate."

"Not that again. I have declared I have yet to accept this. You will provide me duration. I thought this was agreed upon?"

"It was," Omad answered. "Only Darthorn refuses to tarry."

"I understand. He commands you to jump, and you inquire how high? Well, I am not ready as yet. I understand your plight, and I am aware of my chosen destiny. However, I do not accept this and doubt I ever will. I am not your princess, and I can never be.

"You expect me to exist in a land that is heading for certain destruction. It's too much. I'm sorry for your plight, and I pray you locate the strength to overcome Darthorn. Only tis not my fight. I will not be forced into wedlock!"

She was near tears, yet none would come; enough had been shed during the time she had been in Tsinia.

Omad huffed and shuffled his feet. "I recognise your distress, Thya, and I concur with all you declare. Alas, whether you believe this or not, Tsinia is your home and has always been. Even if you depart, you are still the rightful heir. Recall if you will what occurred on your land England. If you are to return, I am convinced your duration will be plagued with attempts to destroy you. Darthorn will not cease. He will continue dispatching Senxs to Earth. Here, you are protected by the employment of your gifts and your loyal subjects. On Earth, you will have naught to protect you. Unless you confront your destiny and aid your kinsmen, you will surely die."

Thya was speechless. *Either way, I lose. Omad is just in his words. Nothing would stop Darthorn from sending more Senxs to kill me, unless I find a way to stop him myself.*

"Depart," she said. "I will dispatch word when I have decided what to do."

Omad stood up. "By your leave." He bowed. "I pray to the Changlins to bestow on you the strength in producing the correct decision."

Kezar watched Omad depart then returned to Thya.

"I sense bad tidings," Kezar said.

"I fear my rest and peace have come to an end. Summon Alkazar to my counsel; I will return to the Recas in waiting."

"At once." Kezar curtsied then ran off in haste.

Thya had barely time to think before Alkazar's quick arrival to the Recas.

"You requested for me, my lady," he said, breathless, as though he had run all the way.

"I did, Alkazar. Sit."

Kezar left, shutting the door behind her.

"I sense the cause of your summons."

"I assumed you would. The moment has arrived. Darthorn will endure not longer and tis the duration to face my doom or continue with the consequence of yours. As I have confessed prior to now, I have a belief, deep in my heart. I understand what I will do, only I cannot accept this. Alkazar, I have not had time to come to terms with my fate. I summon you for advice and hope for consolation. I'm not afraid. The struggle is that I cannot accept the burden. I am not your saviour."

"How I sympathise with you, but such is the responsibility that comes with your standing. You are resolved to proceed?"

"Do not force me to utter such words, yet I realise I am. Do you deem me ready?"

"Unfortunately, you are fit and able. Tis not my standing to state otherwise. Suppose the requirement arises, you retain the power to protect and control yourself; although, I desire longer in session you are well trained. I believe there is more I can absorb from you, a greater strength of your power I have yet to discover. Alas, this will remain so, until your introduction to your future spouse."

"Do not utter such words!" Thya cried. "I will venture to Senx for peace without a union. I will not discuss this proposal, and I believe tis wise to relate Darthorn of this prior to my visit."

"Tis by Darthorn's authority that the alliance is settled with wedlock. Do you consider he would consent to a treaty absent from this?"

"Nay, I do not. Even so, I will attempt it. What other option do I have? He has not yet met with me; he is not acquainted with my charm and persuasion," Thya joked.

Thya noted his forced smile and deep breath of satisfaction.

He nodded. "Then tis set in motion. In any case, a discussion will come to pass, and, as the Oracles have predicted, we will be victorious. I will inform Omad of your resolve. This ought to release the pressure on you. Arrange this instance when you are to encounter, or Darthorn will dictate."

"Very well. One tril moon from the present. I refuse to linger, and I'm resolved to proceed. I desire to put an end to this unpleasantness."

"Tis your command, so be it. We will meditate and consult the Changlins."

Under the guidance and watchful eye of Alkazar, Thya meditated and prayed for strength and guidance.

Alkazar did not sleep well, and his fear for Thya's safety kept him awake through the night. As always, he ran scenarios through his head as his mind raced. He wanted his princess prepared for anything.

"She ought not to partake in the consumption of food and drink," he said, shattering the silence.

Thya spent the next light preparing herself for the confrontation with Darthorn. Pertius gave instructions to her on what she should say and the correct way to behave. He instilled into her the importance of decorum. Alkazar bombarded her with a series of imagined scenarios and instructed her on how to attend to them. By the time they had finished, her mind was reeling. She had barely enough time to visit the Plecky for a short prayer before her departure.

The journey was slow and torturous. To Thya, the mountain seemed to grow with every step. It felt like hours had passed before she saw the black gates of Senx. She prayed for strength, questioning if this was the beginning or the end.

Armed guards escorted Thya through the city. The sight stunned her, though she wasn't quite sure what to expect. She presumed the Senxs would appear vicious, like her escort of guards. To her surprise, the citizens appeared similar to Tsinians. They hurried around, busy with their tasks, yet merry. They were well groomed, and they appeared healthy and happy. It was obvious that no matter what she thought about Darthorn, none could say he wasn't good to his kinsmen.

Thya was led to a large, bare chamber. The hall was made from gold. It glittered and shined, giving the chamber a rich and powerful feel.

The guards withdrew from the chamber without announcement. It was then Thya became aware she was not alone.

On the far-left side of the chamber stood a Senx. His back was to her, and his interest was otherwise occupied as he stared out the window covering most of the wall. It was obvious to Thya who he was, for she had seen him in her dreams. His large hands were clasped behind his back, his stance proud and dominating. He was wearing a long crimson-and-gold gown that reminded her of a kimono. His jet-black hair hung loose down his back, the length almost touching his hands. There was no doubt in her mind. This was Darthorn, the ruler of Senx.

Thya waited for Darthorn to acknowledge her, but soon realised he was not going to. Her patience could hold out no longer. Coughing loudly, she stirred Darthorn from his thoughts. His head whipped around, and his scorn turned into an artificial smile, or so Thya thought.

"Welcome, princess," his deep voice boomed.

It took him four powerful strides to reach her. He extended his arm, which she took, then he led her to the middle of the open-spaced stone floor. With a wave of his hand, a gold, regal-style table and two chairs appeared. The table was laden with fruit and beverages. Thya gasped. Still, the magic of her new world surprised her.

"Be seated," he instructed, pointing to one of the chairs.

As Thya took her seat, Darthorn poured a liquid that looked similar to Tsinian wine into two goblets and handed one to her. Remembering what Alkazar had said, she held the cup in her hands, not daring to let the wine touch her lips.

"I am pleased to lay sight upon you, finally, for I have lingered long for our rendezvous. Your reputation precedes you. Tis an honour you travel to my land."

"I do not concur," Thya retorted.

His eyes turned black, and his face displayed a frightful scowl. Thya stiffened, startled by the abrupt change in his demeanour.

She watched his false smile recover, looking as

though he was taking control of his anger, yet she imagined he wanted to tear her from limb to limb.

Thya recalled Alkazar's words. "If you journey to Senx carrying a stance of arrogance and bravery, then I guarantee you will throw away any hope." It was essential to tread carefully and be aware of her tongue.

"I will permit that to pass," Darthorn said, though it was spoken as a warning. "I do not doubt your subjects have voiced their opinion of me, my evil doings and how loathsome I am." His cruel laughter echoed through the empty chamber. "Do not presume to understand me, Thya. Why heed idle gossip? Judge for yourself. I desire to persuade you of my genuineness. I long to unite in friendship."

Thya doubted his words. She had laid judgement upon him and found him guilty on all accounts. She opened her mouth to speak and then stopped as footsteps approached. Darthorn rose, and Thya, sensing it was polite to follow his example, did the same. Then, not wanting to seem interested in Darthorn's business, she turned away from him.

"Greetings, Father," a clear and soothing voice rang out.

Out of curiosity, Thya turned in the direction of the sound.

Kneeling beside Darthorn was a younger Senx, certainly younger than Thya expected. He possessed hypnotic blue eyes but carried the same discourteous attitude as his father. He rose and acknowledged Thya with a smile that faded when it was not returned. He was handsome, Thya could not deny that, with distinct features and a pleasing face, except she had learnt from experience that looks could be deceiving. Without taking his eyes off her, the boy took Thya's hand and kissed it.

"Tis an honour to lay sight upon you, my lady." He bowed courteously.

She felt a sudden urge to wipe her hand.

"Absolve me for my lateness, Father. I deemed it prudent for you to encounter one another without the burden of my presence."

"I will depart, Kovon." Darthorn turned to address Thya. "Tis inevitable we will encounter one another in passing. When this occurs, I require for us to converse further."

With a swish of his gown, Darthorn left, leaving Kovon and Thya alone.

Kovon sat and turned to address Thya. "I will be direct. I have been impatient for our encounter ever since I was informed of your planned arrival." His smile was sickly sweet and caused her stomach to churn.

"You are fortunate I was able to attend at all. There was an ambush on Earth, an attempt to take my life."

Kovon face was expressionless. "I am rejoiced to sight you well," he finally answered. "Tis desired our wedlock would present union to our great lands. My subjects are as anxious for peace as your own. Sighting you resolves my wait. I have visualised your beauty, and I am pleasured that you exceed my expectations. You are an astounding Ganty, and I am impatient for our union and the alliance to commence."

Thya listened, only she couldn't bear to hear any more. Forgetting Alkazar's warning, she spoke her mind. "Okay, Kovon, you can cease with this charade. I am aware, as are you, what you are truly after, and I am certain tis naught to do with me. You desire Tsinia. You always have and forever will, and the only means to do this is by becoming one with their heir."

Kovon smiled. "Bright as well as beautiful. You have been taught well. Yet why would a union with me be so terrible? I would present to you all you desire."

She watched him lick his lips before slowly approaching her.

Thya stepped back and then laughed. "Well, well, well, the mighty Kovon befallen by a woman. Enlighten me, please. If I bat my eyelashes, will you fall on your knees in worship?" She laughed again. "I do not desire to wed you, Kovon. You repulse me. I would rather subsist in celibacy than allow you to touch me."

"Do not mock me, princess," he warned. "Performance of matrimony is not necessary for me to rule Tsinia. There are additional methods, as you are familiar with."

Thya stood up, feeling the indignation and anger wash over her. "I journeyed in the hope we could build an alliance absent from wedlock and have peace absent from bloodshed. I understand now tis impossible. The Tsinians are desperate to exist, absolved from the wrath of your father. I have bequeathed my word that I will aid them in their struggle, with the exception of a union with you."

"Thya, you do not want to create an enemy out of me. I, too, hope for peace, yet I am convinced you doubt my words. I sense you have resolve of me, and I will not be able to persuade you otherwise."

"I believe our encounter is concluded. Tis obvious you have not the intention of peace, as I will not enter in a union with you; although, I do admit it was gratifying to sight you. I have learnt much, and from what I have observed, tis all genuine."

Kovon stood up. The chair fell to the floor with a crash, making her jump. The dark expression she had seen in Darthorn was displayed on Kovon's face, only something more sinister was present.

"You retain a sharp tongue, Thya. Tis prudent you do not remark more. I recognise the duration spent absent from your land has not taught you manners. Tis prudent you depart. I will permit you duration to mull over your decision, for I know your heart will alter."

Thya clenched her fists. "I do not require duration to mull over your pathetic proposal. You will never control Tsinia, and I will rule henceforth."

She regretted the words immediately. Did she realise what she had said? Would she keep to her word? Could she?

"You will pay for your impertinence," Kovon warned. "What I do hereafter will be on your head. Remember that, princess!"

Thya left then, knowing if she said anything else, her kinsmen would be put in further peril.

Kovon paced up and down the chamber. How dare she address him so? He had never encountered a female Bora with such spirit and stubbornness. She was born a queen, that much was obvious from her regal manner. It was regretful she would not have the opportunity to rule as she intended, for if his father's plan did not transpire, Kovon retained his own preparations for the princess. Why had he permitted her to depart, though? He ought to have imprisoned her; she would not have been able to escape to go back to Tsinia. Nay, his father's games were foolish. If I were warlord, all would bow at my feet. He turned and left the hall.

Darthorn had listened in on the conversation between Thya and his son. It amused him to see Kovon so affected by another. Should he be wary of Thya? Was she an enemy he needed to watch? She was brave, even if that bravery was employed through stupidity. She ought never to have stood up to Kovon. It had been some time since Darthorn had witnessed his son's temper. If Thya understood him, known what he was capable of, Darthorn was certain she would not have confronted him. Nevertheless, the damage was done now. She would soon regret her outburst.

What distressed Darthorn, however, was her announcement on ruling Tsinia. Was it a provoked reaction to the moment, or was she serious about accepting the crown? Jakar had given him the impression Thya wanted naught to do with Tsinia. Only now he understood it differently. He decided to consult the Darkeye about her, and so left without delay.

Darthorn entered the cold, damp cavern. With a wave of his hand, two torches glowed, though the cave was still cloaked in a dark shadow. A light brightened the gloom as the Darkeye acknowledged its master.

He approached the Eye situated on top of a large rock column and placed his hands on either side of the crystal. An image appeared, unclear at first. It became sharper until Darthorn was staring into the face of his enemy. He despised the sight of her yet kept his vision upon the revelation the Eye displayed.

He observed a session between Thya and Alkazar as he mumbled to himself. "So, Thya possesses the gift of Flite. Tis good to acquire yet damaging to my plans."

She was strong-willed, and having conversed with her, Darthorn judged her to be impossible to control. She had developed into a bigger threat than he initially believed. "Curse them for her reinstatement. They will pay for her defiance!"

Darthorn removed his hands from the Darkeye, and the image faded. It once again looked like a harmless gem. There was only one answer, so he spoke the words that even the great Darthorn dreaded to utter.

Omad had been waiting outside the gates of Senx for Thya's return. He was not permitted entrance into the city, and Thya insisted that he wait. Even though he feared for the safety of his princess, he was more worried about his own.

Armed Senxs surrounded him. Omad kept his eyes to the ground, fearful of making direct eye contact with one of the monsters. As time passed, he became agitated. Maybe it wasn't such a good idea to have allowed Thya to go alone unprotected. However,

Darthorn had presented his word she would not be harmed.

Finally, the gates swung open. Thya was escorted by guards down the path towards him. He silently prayed to the Changlins, thanking them for her safe return. From the expression on her face, though, he could surmise the meeting had not gone well. He held out his arm and she grabbed hold of it, pulling him away from the gate in her haste to flee.

They made their way down the treacherous mountain path. It wasn't until the gates of Senx slammed shut behind them that Omad asked Thya the outcome of the meeting.

She gnawed at her bottom lip. "I am so regretful, Omad. I believe matters have worsened. Kovon infuriated me, and I could not permit him to talk to me in such a manner. I declared my true feelings to him and remarked much. More than was meant. I doubt there will ever be an alliance between Tsinia and Senx now."

Omad's expression turned grave. "Let us confer with the council. Amends have to be formed momentarily."

They spoke no more and walked in silence back to Tsinia.

Alkazar worried for Thya's safety and was eager for her return. He paced nervously, unable to concentrate on his studies. Finally, the announcement of her coming rang through the forest. He left immediately, practically jumping down the steps. He arrived in time to see Thya being ushered towards the Escos by Omad.

"You are not summoned for counsel, Alkazar," Omad told him. "And this council does not concern you."

Even with the refusal, Alkazar did not relent. He touched Omad's shoulder and attempted to look over to see inside. "Declare to me, what has occurred?"

The seriousness of Omad's expression concerned him. "The conclusion, I fear, my friend. The conclusion." Then Omad turned and walked sombrely into the Escos. The door shut, leaving him alone, bewildered.

"The conclusion," he repeated, almost in a whisper.

Alkazar sat on the ground. What was meant by that? He deemed the meeting had not run smoothly, though he was certain Thya performed to her finest and was civil enough with her tongue. In the name of the Changlins, what could have gone wrong? Oh, how he desired to transform into a telent, fly into the Escos, and observe what was conversed. He pitied the need for Thya to face her judges alone and decided to wait, no matter how long it would take.

The Dark Force

THE COUNCIL MEETING HAD HARDLY begun when the alarm rang through the city. Thya didn't have to ask its meaning; the councillors terrified expressions told her there was trouble.

They evacuated the Escos in a state of blind panic. Tsinians ran to their dwellings. Some looked lost and confused; others ran aimlessly. Thya stood on the steps of the Escos. Her body still, her eyes looking straight ahead as her mind blanked everything around her.

Alkazar found the Tsinian who sounded the alarm, and his anxiety deepened. "Skayfla, why the alert? Do you perceive something of importance?"

Skayfla possessed the gift of Sonica, heightened hearing. He could hear the slightest sound from afar. "My tidings are grave, Alkazar. Darthorn has assembled an army, and they are marching towards Tsinia. There is something more I fear. He has unleashed the Dark Force. There is a strength, an energy if you will, far greater than any we could comprehend. We must prepare for the attack. May the power of the Changlins be upon you, my friend."

It was worse than Alkazar could have imagined. He was compelled to gather the gifted Tsinians, for only they could protect them now. His desire to learn what had been conversed in Senx grew. What had occurred for Darthorn to alter his character so dramatically?

There was no need to look for the gifted Tsinians because they sought him out. They understood they were needed as they had played their role many times before. The group also included Thya, who, now that she had completed her studies, could use her skills to the fullest. Even so, Alkazar was not pleased with having her so close to the attack line. If the Senx saw her standing among them, she would be their first target – their only target. However, he could not argue with the council's command or deny the strength of her gift.

Alkazar tried to understand the reason for the attack. Though he would never trust Darthorn or any Senx, he pondered the sudden transformation. One moment he required peace, and the next he was dispatching an army to destroy them. Why?

Fear rose in the hearts of the Tsinians. Alkazar observed Thya, who stood close beside him. There was no fear in her eyes, no panic, only blankness, as if she had cut herself off from everyone and everything.

Omad ordered all the Tsinians, apart from Alkazar's assembled group, to leave the city and head for the border of their land until it was safe to return. Words of hope were called out to the group as the villagers departed. The remainder stood in silence to wait.

Alkazar had the task of electing the gift to use in their defence and how to employ the gift. Only, he could not do this until he knew how big the assault would be. The suddenness of the attack gave him little time to plan his strategy. Even so, he had yet to fail his kinsmen.

His mind again raced through possible scenarios and came up with a counterattack for each. Fortunately, the gathering did not have long to wait. They heard the sound of a hundred soldiers marching towards them, and they were soon able to sight them.

Their enemy was clad in black leather garments, with silver chainmail and gold armour covering their chests and arms. Each carried a shield and a sword, which they held at chest height as they advanced.

When the last of the soldiers came into view, the

first were almost upon the city. Alkazar chose their defence quickly.

"Grenko," he called, "produce a growth of thorns and thistle around our borders. An enclosure sturdy and firm so it will deny them admission."

Grenko stepped forward. He squeezed his eyes shut; his head bowed. He made an action with his hands, as though he was sprinkling something on the ground. Instantly, a hedge of thorns and thistles sprouted from the earth before the Senx. Soon, it became larger than the tallest Tsinian. The group watched as the Senxs tried to hack and chop their way through, only to no avail. Those who attempted to cut their way through screamed when the thorns pierced their armour and cut into their skin. These were no ordinary thorns; they were as sharp as knives. No protection could have aided the soldiers. After a time, the warriors started to withdraw.

"Nay, this is too effortless," Alkazar called out in alarm. "Why do they retreat? They are recalled for a purpose. Preserve and be aware."

As they watched, a portion of the hedge crumpled, as if crushed by an invisible force.

"What the blazes?" Alkazar cursed.

The Tsinians backed away. The invisible energy proceeded onwards, flattening everything in its path. The Dark Force contained such strength that the Tsinians doubted anything could put an end to its destruction. Turning from its path, it started towards the Plecky.

Alkazar watched in horror as the force smashed the roof of the Plecky. The building caved inwards, burying the sacred Changlins. The Tsinians scattered, fearful of being hit by flying debris. They waited for Alkazar's command. Once the Plecky had been destroyed, the Dark Force started towards the Escos, destroying every tree dwelling in its path.

Transfixed by the spectacle, his eyes tried to comprehend what they were seeing.

"Do something, Alkazar!" Thya screamed.

Thya's cry awoke him from his trance.

"Maril," he called out.

Maril possessed the gift of Freice, the ability to freeze an object, though unfortunately not a person nor beast. He didn't need Alkazar to tell him what to do. He stood as close as was safe, raised his arms into the air, and pointed his fingers to the sky. Then, with his fists clenched, he pointed his thumbs towards where he thought the Force would be.

"Focus, Maril," Alkazar instructed.

Nothing happened.

Maril dropped his hands to his side in defeat. "The energy is substantial. I do not possess sufficient strength."

The Force was nearly upon the Escos.

"My lady," he called. "Thya!" Alkazar shouted a second time.

She heard the second call and walked over to where Alkazar stood.

"Take up with Maril. I require you to concentrate. Disregard your gift of Flite. When you reach the Owto, command your energy to freeze the Force."

"I do not possess the gift of Freice, only Maril —"

Alkazar spoke gently. "Trust me."

Thya was puzzled by his request. Even so, she stood beside the bewildered Maril and focused on the invisible Force settling over the Escos. Once she'd reached the Owto, a hidden voice she hadn't met before instructed her on thoughts and commands. Thya concentrated, and so intense was her attention she didn't see what happened.

From the ground upwards, ice appeared. It grew with speed and froze the energy just as the Dark Force was about to crush the roof of the Escos.

There were no cheers, only a hushed silence followed by questions: How? What? When?

Thya recovered from her trance, startled by the sight of the monstrous lump of ice before her.

"My lady," Alkazar called, "I entrust the final destruction in your capable hands."

Using her gift of Flite, she toppled the frozen mass of energy. It crashed into the mountain, shattering into thousands of pieces. The group cheered loudly, chanting their princess's name. Alkazar silenced them.

"My dear friends, I beg you be silent to what you witnessed. I require conversation with our lady prior to the occurrence being announced. Do I hold your assurance?"

"With certainty," they answered.

It was agreed that Maril had frozen the invisible force and that Thya participated in the final destruction only.

Thya was confused and frightened by Alkazar's words. Once again, she felt vulnerable and scared.

Those sent to the borders returned upon hearing word of the thwarted attack on their city. All were disturbed by the devastation.

Omad and the council ran to where the Plecky once stood and removed the rubble in haste, desperate to find the damaged Changlins. Omad rejoiced loudly when he came upon them. "Praise to the Changlins! They are untouched."

"With certainty," Alkazar answered. "The Changlins cannot be destroyed. Buried certainly, yet you would still sight them untouched. By your leave, I will escort the princess back to the Recas. She is weak from the employment of her gift, for it was our lady who fell the Dark Force."

Omad bowed down to her. "Well, then, my lady, we are indebted to you."

"'Tis my duty to aid my kinsmen. Is that not what I was brought back to do?"

"Well voiced, my lady, and so you have. Withdraw and rest. My gratitude goes with you."

As weak as she was, Thya would not leave. "I

apologise for what has occurred in your city. I realise that I am the cause of this destruction. I will remain and aid you in rebuilding it, then for your sake, you ought to return me to Earth. You are safer absent from my presence. I do not hold a fondness for your land, and I would like to return home. I beg you to permit me to depart; it would be prudent for all."

Omad dusted off his clothes. "Do not concern yourself, my lady. Buildings can be restored. Our existence cannot. I worry that the Dark Force will recur whether you are among us or not. You ought to understand why we require an alliance."

Thya was shocked. "You require an alliance after all that has occurred? Are you mad? What will it take for you to realise tis not the means?"

Her raised voice was heard above the noise of rocks and ice being thrown aside. The villagers stopped working and listened.

"Why don't you just hand Tsinia over to your enemy?" Thya shouted. "Alliance or not, once Darthorn has a hold he will never release it, and you will be deprived of everything. Do you not understand this?"

"We do not retain another option, my lady." Omad held his hands out in a calming gesture.

"Is there not another means? Why not fight? At least if you are defeated, you can hold your heads with dignity and remark that you attempted, rather than present Tsinia without resistance."

"We follow the prophecy of the Oracles," Omad said. "They revealed that you will deliver us from Darthorn's wrath. Although this is not the correct situation to inquire, I will. How will you aid us, if not by an alliance?"

Thya had no answer for him. She noticed everyone waiting for her response.

"Look at me! Do I appear as a saviour? Did not the Oracles prophecise my departure? Because that is exactly what I am going to do."

She stormed off, blinded by anger. She did not know where she was going or even hear Alkazar calling to her. She felt someone grab her arm and spun to confront the culprit. "Go away, Alkazar. Permit me my solitude."

He ignored her and kept hold of her arm. "You are not to blame for this occurrence. I am convinced you did all you could."

"Well, you are in error then, aren't you? I journeyed to Senx with anger in my heart, the opposite of what you had instructed."

"I do not doubt this, only I am confident you were provoked."

"With certainty. Only do not create justification for me. I caused this destruction. My stubbornness brought ruin to your city, and I am so regretful," she cried.

Alkazar stepped forward to console her, but Thya backed away. "I do not require your pity. Return to

Siren, for I am confident she seeks you. I did not summon for your counsel."

"I did not pursue you out of pity," he growled. "You are selfish, Thya. You retain gifts and possess a power we can only dream of. Tis a precious gift. You retain the fortune to become a heroine and to rule our land, one that is rich and bountiful. In its place, you are resolved to whine and feel regretful for yourself. Certainly, tis written that you are our hope, only I wonder if you serve the purpose."

Alkazar's words cut through Thya's heart like icy knives. The blow almost made her unsteady on her feet. She bowed her head, unable to look him in the eye.

"Nay, Thya," his voice calmed. "I do not pity you. I envy you." He turned away from her.

"Alkazar, wait," she begged. "I am so ashamed." He stopped yet did not turn. "You are just in your words. I have been selfish. All that has been in my thoughts is my fear and woe, not that of my kinsmen's terror. I understand that my return caused great relief and that all I have displayed since is care for myself. I will uncover a means to obtain peace. This I owe you all. I will make amends.

"We have a remark in England: It's cruel to be kind. Only, do not despise me, Alkazar. I am in need of you."

He turned to face her.

"Nay, my lady. You are my queen, even though the

crown has not yet passed into your hands. I will always love you as my queen. I am at your service, and as your servant, permit me to escort you to your home as I am doubtful you can stand much longer."

Thya had forgotten about her fatigue. As if his words cast a spell, she suddenly felt weak. Alkazar was by her side before she swooned. He lifted her into his arms.

"Absolve me, Alkazar," she muttered.

"Hush, my lady."

I am unhappy with myself for causing her such distress. I did not want to be so mean. My words should never have been uttered. I wish I could transport her away from her pain and fears; alas, this can never be. She has to accept and confront her fate, and when she does, it would surely result in her departure, whether to Senx or Earth. No scenario exists that would allow Thya and I to be joined together, regardless of the love I feel for her, and not just as my queen. I have fallen in love with Thya, the woman. One who I know is forbidden and dangerous. Oh, how am I to deal with this?

He carried Thya back to the Recas in silence, leaving instructions with Kezar for Thya to sleep undisturbed. He wanted to stay and watch over her, yet he was needed elsewhere. The Dark Force had destroyed the Plecky and many tree dwellings. There was a lot of work to do, and every hand was required.

Once Thya was sleeping, Alkazar left.

The Tsinians spent the rest of the fading light clearing the rubble. Everyone aided, apart from Kezar, who remained with her mistress. They took the pieces of the frozen Force and placed them in a heap at the base of the mountain in front of the entrance into Tsinia, building a wall that finally separated the two lands. It would serve as a reminder to Darthorn he had, yet again, failed in his quest.

Although significant damage had been done, the Tsinians' hearts were light, and they sang while they worked. They were relieved that not one of their friends had been hurt and they had defeated the dark warlord again. Even with Thya's harsh words and the threat of war seeming greater than before, they still felt Thya was their saviour. With her aid, they could conquer any strength or power Darthorn unleashed upon them. Of course, none save the select group knew of or had witnessed Thya's powers.

Thya woke late in the evening. Refreshed from her deep sleep, she immediately sensed someone else in the room. She turned to find Valcan seated beside her bed. Next to him on the small table was a dish of steaming water with a strong, flowery fragrance.

"I deem tis wise to arouse you, my lady," Valcan said. "Tis late, and you need to consume this if you are to retain your strength."

Thya sat up and took the bowl Valcan held out to her. "Kezar has advised me on your delight in this strange food; although, I cannot understand the reason."

Thya looked down at the thick, orange liquid. "Tomato soup. Actually, tis delicious."

"Prior to devouring this, I require you to receive my treatment."

Valcan spooned some of the fragrant water into a ladle and brought it to her lips. Thya was cautious about drinking it as it looked too hot. However, she trusted Valcan and sipped the liquid. To her relief, it tasted of berries and spices. No sooner had she swallowed the liquid did she felt a warm, soothing sensation fill her being.

"Take nourishment," Valcan instructed. He watched Thya drink the soup with relish. "Alkazar has assured me that your strength was absorbed by the employment of your gift, only I am not so easily fooled. Never have I happened upon the symptoms you exhibit as a result of our gifts. I suppose something variant drained your strength. I would be obliged if you would enlighten me on what this variant is."

"If I understood this, I would declare it to you. Alkazar has yet to converse with me upon this subject. I, too, am anxious to comprehend what occurred. However, enlighten me, Valcan. I woke feeling like I could continue my slumber forever, yet since partaking of this water, I have regained my energy and strength. What is it?"

Valcan smiled. "An exceptional vegetation belonging to our forest. The flower revives one's strength." He grinned. "Though I possess the gift of healing, I retain an interest in natural medicine. If you maintain this between us, I prefer this employment. I forbid you to continue your studies for at least one tril moon, nor do I allow you the employment of your newly found energy. Complete rest. Is that understood?"

"Certainly," she replied. "Again, I owe you my gratitude."

"'Tis Alkazar's concern that brought me to you, for I did not retain awareness of your fatigue. Nonetheless, I am your servant, as always, and will appear whenever I am called upon."

"Valcan, summon Alkazar, please."

"Very well. Only heed my instruction to rest. I will be upset if I am summoned in the cause of your lack of regard." He bowed then left.

Kezar came in after Valcan's departure and cleared away the bowl, then made sure her mistress was in resting attire before retiring herself.

The light came, bringing with it glorious sunshine. Thya was forbidden to leave her bed and so spent most of her time deep in thought. A rap on the chamber door both aroused her and announced Alkazar's arrival.

"Enter," Thya called out.

Alkazar approached her bed. "I was uncertain as to

whether you would be in slumber. My apologies for my lateness. I deemed it prudent to rest and bathe prior to my appearance, as I was not fit to visit myself upon you."

"Oh, Alkazar, absolve me. I had forgotten. Sit, for you are exhausted. Is there much damage?"

"Alas, there is, though there would be a greater extent if it were not for you. Many dwellings were destroyed, but they can be rebuilt. The foundations of the Plecky are being developed as we converse. It will not take a long duration for Tsinia to recover from the attack. We have existed through worse."

Thya shook her head. "I am unclear. You state it is because of me the Dark Force was destroyed, yet how can that be? I do not recall. I cannot comprehend how I aided. Will you explain this to me?"

"I will but be patient because I am still uncertain. Until we continue with our sessions, I cannot be confident of my judgement."

"Very well."

"There is another gift a Ganty could possess, though tis seldom conversed of. The gift is Yepsy. Tis the most powerful of all gifts, the ability to control the forces of nature: earth, fire, water, air, and spirit. And they are capable of directing the weather." Alkazar stopped then, hoping Thya would deduce what he was trying to tell her.

"You mean the Changlins."

"With certainty." He smiled. "The power of the Changlins could be bestowed to this Ganty."

Thya swallowed hard. "And you believe I possess this power?"

"Without complete evidence, I will not respond. I am aware of your strong connection to the Changlins and have sensed a strange energy around you, dissimilar to others. I have always believed you to be of unique power, only I am uncertain as to what or why. I have sighted your ability, and I am even more convinced of my hypothesis.

"Why have you not conversed of this sooner?"

"The gift is extraordinary. My generation has not yet witnessed a Ganty who possesses Yepsy. I had my suspicions, only I desired to set them to practice prior to expressing them. I apologise for placing you in that position without your awareness. It was thoughtless and dangerous. Absolve me, my lady?" He took her hand and looked into her eyes.

"You are absolved," Thya said. "So, with Yepsy, how is it I retained the ability to Freice?"

"You control the forces of nature – wind, rain, and ice – which is why you were able to freeze the Dark Force. I understand this is all new, strange, and maybe scary for you; nevertheless, I will do my utmost to answer all your questions."

This was too much for Thya to take in. She removed her hand from his and played with her hair.

Alkazar watched her silently, yet he understood her thoughts.

"You state you require evidence," Thya asked. "What evidence?"

"'Tis necessary to be in session, only Valcan has deemed you unfit to regress."

"And if I announce to you that I am fit and able, who will you abide by?"

"Very well. Only if you tire will I conclude the session and not be accountable for your condition. You are a stubborn Tsinian, Thya." He grinned.

She felt the same sexual desires building up, only knowing how important the session was could she push them aside and concentrate on reaching the Owto.

"Have you not gazed out of a window and longed for the rain to diminish? Desired for it to cease?"

"Certainly."

"I require you to do similar, except you will demand that it rains only outside this window. You will desire this more than you have desired anything. Is this understood?"

Thya nodded.

Alkazar walked to the small, arched window and looked out. The sky was clear, not a storm cloud in sight.

"Concentrate, Thya," he instructed. "Vision a bright, searing morn. The heat is beating down, and you feel discomforted. What you require is rain.

Rivers of cool rain. You desire this more than anything."

A few drops of rain pattered onto the marble window ledge. Alkazar could not believe what he was seeing. "Demand it to rain," he called with excitement. "'Tis your command."

The clouds opened, and the water came down in force.

"Amazing," he whispered, spellbound by the sight. The rain gushed just outside the window. On either side of it, the ground was dry, as though there was an invisible force field.

Eventually, he dragged his eyes away from the window and back to Thya. For just a moment, he was sure her eyes had turned white. He blinked. When he looked again, they were her normal colour.

"Thya, come sight what you created."

On the call of her name, Thya came back to reality. She attempted to get off the bed, only she was too weak.

"'Tis what I warned you about," he scolded.

Thya frowned and lifted her arms out to Alkazar. He helped her to the window, and she looked at the soggy ground. Still, the rain fell.

"Did I really do that?"

Alkazar laughed.

She held onto him tightly as they watched. A chill crept over her, a fear of the power she witnessed. She felt safe in his arms, as if nothing could harm her, and more importantly, she couldn't do harm.

Although Alkazar was eager to learn more of her power, he would not probe further until he deemed her fit and well. This did not stop him spending every waking moment with her, at least until Valcan put an end to his visits. Alkazar had seen how drained she became and was prepared to wait until he was certain she could cope with the sessions. Three tril moons passed before they continued.

Over the next weeks, Thya and Alkazar learnt and tested her power in secrecy. It was difficult for Thya to take command of it at first. However, with Alkazar's patience and talent as a tutor, she eventually mastered her gift.

While Thya pushed herself to the limits, Alkazar noticed that twice when he had brought her to the Owto, he had lost connection with her and had a hard time bringing her back. He didn't know why it happened, and it scared him. He needed to find out where she went, how far she had gone, and, most importantly, why they had lost their connection.

Things were quiet in Senx, and Alkazar was continually surprised by how far her talents reached.

Both studied hard. Thya learning about the code and her gift, and Alkazar trying to discover more about Thya's strange powers. As they spent time together, their bodies seemed to react like a magnet. Thya's skin tingled every time Alkazar looked at her, and both felt a sudden need when they were apart. With awkward grins and smiles, and gentle touches and flirting banter. Thya's body mind and soul wanted Alkazar, which confused her, knowing it was wrong but feeling it was so right.

Thya took the time to explore Tsinia further, especially when she felt the need for solitude.

Thya had walked for miles through her land. On one such walk she came to a place she had not yet visited. In front of her stood a mountain of rock, and it seemed like a dead end at first sight. However, looking closer, she noticed a small crack large enough for her to slip through. She worried if going farther meant leaving the Tsinian borders, but curiosity got the better of her. Although the crack was narrow, she squeezed through and was astounded by what awaited her.

Moss-covered rocks enclosed a crystal blue lake. Not a dwelling could be sighted. At last, a place where she could be alone. She breathed a sigh of satisfaction and made her way down to the water. It was a humid afternoon, and she felt the sudden need for a swim. She checked to make sure no one was about before undressing.

As soon as her foot entered the cool water, she felt refreshed, so she dived into the lake, hoping the rest of her body would be given vigour. It was as if the water cast a spell, for her cares were immediately forgotten. She swam contently, up and down the lake, gliding on the surface. Her thoughts left her; all the memories of the past weeks forgotten.

Alkazar, too, felt the need for solitude and had unknowingly followed Thya's path. It was not the first time he had been to the lake. He swam in the waters many a time when he needed to relax his thoughts, only he was startled to hear a sweet voice singing. He was curious to discover who it was who interrupted his solitude.

He approached quietly. The melody enchanted him, and he became more anxious to hear it better than to discover who was singing. He crouched behind a rock. Instead of peering over, he sat, eyes closed, content to listen to the voice. When the song ended, he opened his eyes, surprised. It was as if he had been hypnotised. He felt drowsy yet comforted. His curiosity stirred within, and he peered over the top of the rock, stifling a gasp.

Thya's naked form glided through the water. It was then, at that very moment, when he realised they would become one.

Feeling an urgent need to talk to her, he was about to stand up and call to her, but common sense took over. He continued to watch until she stepped out and dressed.

He crept away some distance then walked towards the lake, whistling loudly.

Thya heard his whistle and hurried to dress. Surprised someone was about, she decided to meet with them.

"My lady pardon the intrusion. I was not aware of your presence," Alkazar greeted.

"I presumed I was alone. I required solitude."

"Then absolve me for my intrusion. I will depart."

"Nay, stay. I am quite satisfied. In fact, I am gladdened by your presence."

She smiled at him. Alkazar struggled to control the thoughts racing through his mind.

"I was led to believe there was not a location in Tsinia that was without eyes."

"'Tis so. Few hold awareness of this location as few would journey out of our borders. I come when I require solitude, for tis tranquil."

"I agree. I feel relaxed. Only I'll remember in future to be more cautious." She blushed. "It did not occur to me others could travel. I was too carefree."

Alkazar did his best to hide his embarrassment. "As I remarked, few are aware of this location. Do not allow this to interfere with your leisure. The spring contains healing properties. It does well to bathe in it."

"I believed as much," Thya said. "It was as though

I was somewhere else. I believe I could have floated out of my being I was so relaxed."

Alkazar laughed. "'Tis an ingredient in one of Valcan's many remedies."

"Ah, so that is his secret." She laughed. "I will definitely be more aware of where I select to swim."

"I bestow my service to you, Thya. If you desire to return, I will accompany you and retain watch so your swim will not be disturbed."

"That is gracious of you, Alkazar. I will hold you to that."

They talked some more about Thya's life on Earth. She noticed how attentive he was to everything she said, and she could imagine his amazement if he ever stepped foot on Earth. When the sky began to change colour, Alkazar suggested they return.

A New Warlord Reigns

SINCE THE EMBARRASSING DEFEAT OF the Dark Force's invisible energy, Darthorn preferred to stay away from the Eye. In fact, it had been a long time since he'd set foot inside the cavern. He decided to take Tsinia without the aid of the Dark Force. The fact he had tried numerous times before did not seem to concern him. Darthorn was certain his plan would succeed and that this time, he would be victorious. He'd been planning his assault for a month and was confident it would have the desired result.

He was a great warlord and would not be defeated. He possessed the power of the Darkeye and retained the greatest army in all of Enunac, so why could he not eliminate this one particular Bora? She made him look weak and powerless. His kinsmen would lose respect if he did not free himself from her. She would not be triumphant this time. Darthorn would show her how forceful a warlord he could be. He would not sight defeat.

Yet even with his army prepared and ready for action, Darthorn felt the need for the Darkeye's guidance. He wanted to vision his victory before it happened. To gloat on what would be before it became. Be warned of any unexpected or misguided actions by his interfering enemies.

The Darkeye acknowledged its master by glowing brightly. Darthorn placed both hands on the crystal. The vision, at first blurry, became clearer, only it concerned Darthorn greatly. Where were his soldiers? Where were the chained Tsinians?

His enemy, Thya, slept upon a bed in a chamber Darthorn presumed was her own. Her eyes widened with horror. Her face expressed such terror it actually startled him. She gasped for breath, and a smile appeared on his. It was over in a matter of moments. Thya's lifeless body lay limp across the bed. Her arms dangled over the edge and her eyes remained open, showing her final moments of immense terror. She was dead. There was not a doubt in his mind. Only where was the onslaught? It was as though an invisible hand had smothered her face, causing her to suffocate. The vision faded, and the Darkeye was once again a harmless black crystal.

"Is this a vision of the future or what could be?" he asked, hoping the Darkeye would answer his question. Deep in his soul, he knew where he could get the answer he yearned, only could he risk calling upon the Dark Force again? His enemy was dead, taken without a struggle. Oh, if only it were that effortless. There was only one way to find out, so he uttered the sacred words.

Kovon had been interrogating Jakar on Thya's movements, learning nothing new. She seemed t spend her time between meditation, sessions, and solitude. How exciting, Kovon thought sarcastically. He was secretly eager to meet with her again. She infuriated him, yet it was a pleasant sensation. Never had a Bora, and a female one at that, talked down to him. Thya was not afraid. She had the courage to stand up to him, and Kovon relished their next rendezvous.

His father was at last content and satisfied with the planned onslaught. The great army of Senx was set for battle. All Darthorn had to do was to give the order. Kovon had given himself the authority to lead them into battle; his thirst for action left him dry. He was keen to see Thya again, the contemplation of her on bended knees, bound and enslaved and begging for his mercy, appealed to him. Someone as ravishing as her at his beck and call was a fantasy, and he was impatient to act it out.

After dismissing the exhausted Jakar, Kovon went in search of his father. He was desperate to know when Darthorn planned to strike his blow upon Tsinia.

Kovon searched most of the chambers and found them to be empty. It then occurred to him that he might find his father in the cavern seeking advice from the Darkeye. Knowing he could not enter the cavern, he stood outside. He was about to call to Darthorn when he heard his father answering another. He understood the warlord was consulting the Dark Force, whose voice was audible to its master only. With no desire to learn the dark ways, he was about to walk off when he heard his father speak his name. His interest awoken, he leaned in closer.

"You vow that her existence will be removed? There is no doubt of this?"

Kovon did not hear the reply.

"Much could go awry. Why ought I accept what you have displayed? That it is certain? Was that not a vision of what could occur? I understand. I will consider your proposition, only tis such a great sacrifice. You cannot demand my pronouncement this instant. He is my only son!"

Darthorn's words hit Kovon like a jagged spear piercing his stomach.

"She is, only," Darthorn continued. "This is understood, certainly. Nevertheless, is there not another direction? Why Kovon? He is the only heir of

Senx. Tis true. I have consumed my existence attempting to control Tsinia and the power of the Changlins. I will do whatever is requested. However, do not demand this of me, I beseech you. When I cease to exist, who will be present to reign over Senx?" There was a long pause. "I did not envision this. A new Genesis, and I would be the father of a new race of Boras, half Tsinian and half Senx. I will become the sovereign and master of all. How soon after the demise of Kovon will Thya's breath be seized? Tis good, and you do not foresee any alteration? Thya will be dead. This is a certainty?" Darthorn paused again. "Very well. It will be as you requested," he announced. "The soul of Kovon for the demise of Thya and possession of the power of the Changlins. Finally, I will acquire Tsinia," Darthorn declared.

Kovon's legs buckled beneath him. He fell to the cold, stone ground, stunned by his father's agreement with the Dark Force. Surely, he was mistaken. His father would never agree to this. Only he had heard the deadly pact for himself. Kovon stood up, his weakness diminished as vengeance flowed through him.

"Very well, Father. If this is the approach you demand, let the games commence. Tis period for alteration. Senx will retain a new ruler, and we will soon sight who will command Tsinia."

While Darthorn spent his time devising how to kill

his son, Kovon spent his time planning the unexpected demise of his father.

Darthorn had no intent to delay the inevitable. His method, a little poison in and around Kovon's cup. None would be wise. Who would dare to suspect the warlord of foul play? Kovon was due any moment, and Darthorn felt nervous. It was all within his grasp. Why did the Force not convey this solution previously? It was effortless. He cursed for waiting so long.

Kovon entered. "Father," he greeted.

They embraced each other, lingering longer than usual, knowing it would be their last embrace. They sat facing one another. Darthorn poured the wine. Nothing strange about that, for he had done it most evenings. It was a ritual for them, a moment to enjoy the coming evening and discuss the passing light.

"A toast," Darthorn announced. "To your approaching wedlock."

Kovon raised his cup to his lips then paused. Darthorn's eyes followed.

"How I desire for this," Kovon remarked. "Do you speculate an adjustment of mind, Father? She is stubborn, though I would gain pleasure in taming her."

Darthorn laughed falsely. "So, a toast… in educating Princess Thya."

They both laughed and touched cups. Darthorn drank, but to his dismay, Kovon kept his cup close in his hands. Darthorn sensed something was worrying his son and realised he would have to play the caring parent one last time.

"What troubles you, my son? Express frankly." Darthorn's concern was evident.

Kovon sighed. "I am irritated with myself for not dealing with her insolence. Why did I permit a Bora, a Tsinian, to converse with me in such a manner? I ought not to have tolerated it. I ought to have taught her manners directly." Forgetting that his father was present, he continued, "Nonetheless, I will display to her and to all. I will force them to quake in fear of the name Kovon. Not one will regard me with disrespect. Thya will suffer for her words as will all who defy me. I will compel her to beseech for mercy. All will bow in my presence. I will become the greatest warlord that ever existed."

He stopped and stared into his father's pale, shocked face. "Absolve me, for my foolish tongue." Kovon smiled smugly. "Reveal to me, Father. What would you sacrifice to receive what you deemed you rightly deserved?"

Still shocked by his son's speech and more so by the strange and disturbing question, Darthorn thought hard.

"Perhaps… flesh and blood," Kovon answered for him. "At what extent would you willingly participate, Father?"

Darthorn swallowed hard before speaking. "You

have witnessed that I have done just so and will continue to. If the Dark Force commands this of me, then tis a sacrifice I will commit to. You ought to expect to vanquish something precious in return for greatness. You will gain an understanding about this when it is your spell to reign."

To Darthorn's dismay, the conversation did not end there.

"If I were to sacrifice my most cherished possession, it would be you, as there is naught of greater value than my father's love."

Darthorn shifted uncomfortably in his chair. "The issue is, could you? Would you?"

"Nay," Kovon spat as he glared into Darthorn's eyes. "Would you sacrifice your only kin, your flesh and blood for the sake of greatness?"

The conversation had grown far too intense for Darthorn. "All I possess, all of Senx, will eventually become yours. You are the only son and heir of Darthorn. Why would I surrender my heir? It would be for naught, an act of stupidity. Let us drink and continue our conversation in a happier intonation," Darthorn suggested. Thinking the conversation was over, he lifted his cup and drank. Kovon did not.

Kovon smiled. "The wine is not to my palate, Father."

Darthorn slammed his cup on the table, spilling the wine onto the wood. Kovon laughed aloud, happy that his father had at last caught on.

"How could you retain anticipation of my intent?" Darthorn growled. His tone softened slightly. "What would you undertake if you were in my situation, son?" Kovon cringed at the word. "If you held the enemy in the palm of your hand and only one Bora stood on your course, reveal to me your resolve."

"I would crush them. Like father, like son." Kovon laughed cruelly.

Darthorn felt a pressing sensation on his temples. Unable to shake off the feeling that seemed to fill his whole being, he stood up from his chair and walked to the balcony. Not being able to stop the Force pushing him along, he climbed onto the ledge and looked down. Though he had no control over his body, his thoughts were his own. He silently screamed in terror.

Kovon stood behind his father, concentrating hard, his mind clear of all thoughts apart from what he demanded from his subject.

With his gift of Traking, Kovon could control other Boras' minds and make them do things against their will. It came in handy when he wanted the company of the opposite sex. It was easier for the females to be controlled, rather than him knowing they didn't want to be there. He wasn't ugly; far from it. He was handsome, and he knew it, only he was known as a sadist when it came to sex. He preferred the company to enjoy his way of lovemaking, whether they wanted to or not. It had taken many years for him to perfect his talents. Through all his life, he had not encountered an opponent who could resist him.

Even the great Darthorn could not resist.

He was invincible. Not a single foe could destroy him.

Kovon forced his father to look into his eyes, releasing his will just enough to sight the terror upon Darthorn's face.

"Farewell, Father."

He strengthened his will, and Darthorn silently stepped off the edge.

It was in the early light that a Tsinian by the name of Spacia found Darthorn's crushed and mangled body at the foot of the mountain. Her scream rang through the forest, waking all save the dead. A crowd gathered to regard the body of their feared enemy. It was Jakar who, on seeing his master's body, ran to notify Kovon that he was now the warlord of Senx. Guards were sent to retrieve Darthorn's body, and he was laid to rest with honours befitting a warlord.

Kovon was eager to take up the role, for he had many plans.

He would permit his subjects to grieve for the loss of their precious master, after which they would labour for the first duration in their miserable existence.

On seeing and hearing of the death of Darthorn, the citizens of Tsinia rejoiced, but at the request of Thya, the council banned any open celebration; all were behind closed doors. Thya felt it was just, in respect for Kovon's mourning. She even sent him a token, a gesture of good faith, which he ignored.

Three tril moons had passed when Thya was requested to attend the council at the Escos. They were all seated by the time she arrived. Omad motioned for her to approach the addressing star.

"Greetings, my lady." Omad's grin stretched from ear to ear. He was happier than she had seen him for some time. "We are delighted by the turn of events, as I believe you are. The prophecy has been fulfilled, yet we are unsure how you worked into the equation. Nonetheless, Darthorn is deceased, and the threat is obsolete. We can conclusively exist in peace. We, the citizens of Tsinia, cannot demonstrate our gratitude to you. You have been patient with us and revised hard in both the arts and our sacred code. For this, we will regretfully return you to the land you deem to miss."

Thya knew she should feel grateful and relieved by the news. However, she was not.

Omad continued, "Regardless, we beg of you one final request." Thya listened closely, curious as to what it may be. "Kovon seeks an encounter with you again, and he holds for your response."

"After all that has occurred, you would presently

consent to an alliance. I will not ever understand your manner of thought," Thya said, shocked.

"Nay, my lady. Kovon does not express for an alliance. Only of friendship."

"And you believe this? He expects your princess to jump when he commands it. I refuse to comply with his demand. Once was enough. I am gratified you permit my return home; only can you be so definite that receiving Kovon as the new warlord of Senx will not result in your suffering? How can you be convinced he will not attempt to obtain Tsinia by force? I have encountered with him on one occasion, and I believe him to possess the capabilities and conviction to do just that. I notice you all delight in Darthorn's demise, yet I am troubled. I believe Senx has developed into a larger threat than previously."

Omad looked uncomfortable with her news. Zarc rose from his seat. "I fathom your uneasiness, though you ought not to concern yourself further."

Thya was livid.

"How dare you state tis not a concern of mine? You abduct me from my home, forcing me to exist in your world. You rotate my being, and everything I comprehend as truth becomes a lie. You then have the audacity to demand I unite with a vile and evil warlord, require me to master a power I never recognised I possessed, and memorise your code. In return, you hold the nerve to sit there and declare it is naught of my business how you manage my realm."

Thya was so angry she could speak no more. Zarc was about to respond when Omad stood up and silenced him. "I express regret for the councillor's tongue. I am confident it was not meant. You will forever be involved with the concerns of Tsinia, and I hold your statement seriously. I will consider your apprehension. What our friend Zarc was attempting to convey, yet not in a suitable manner, was that we believe there will be harmony within our nation henceforth and that you ought not to agitate yourself with concerns that will not be."

"Fine! Allow me to inform you, one and all. Do not seek my aid, which I judge you will soon require. You appear to believe you can govern finer than a Ganty, then I surrender her to you. Enjoy your democracy. Only, do not seek my guidance when you discover you cannot cope unaided. I expect to depart from Tsinia in one tril moon."

She turned and stormed out of the Escos.

Omad tried to reason with the council. It was not wise to return Thya. He was certain her words were just and presumed Thya felt as though she was being pushed out of her new home, just as she was beginning to settle down and take up her duties. He further believed this would have resulted in her accepting the crown. Only, suddenly, everything had shattered like glass. The trust he had built up with her, the friendship, was ruined. He vowed to repair the damage before her departure. She would not leave her land on bad terms. Omad was adamant about that.

The council, however, would not take him earnestly. Thya had done the task she was brought to do. She had saved her kinsmen as prophesied, and, as she refused to accept the crown, they considered further contribution from her unnecessary.

Omad's mind was made up when Athron woke him from his rest to demand an emergency council and requested Thya attend. Alkazar refused to be left in the dark again. Luckily, she summoned him to her counsel.

Thya was the first to speak. "I can only presume I have been summoned for reason of an Oracle, and that it is of my concern."

"With certainty, my lady," Athron answered.

"Very well, Athron. You are permitted to interpret," she said.

"The swan will fly, the feathers will fall, conversion will not do at all," Athron announced.

"Rephrase," Thya commanded.

"I believe you have been wronged and that we are further away from your acceptance of the crown than ever. I am not familiar with what has been conversed since the downfall of Darthorn. However, I am convinced if you depart from our nation prior to the prophecy being fulfilled, then all of Tsinia and those who exist within her borders will perish. For tis written, so it will be."

"What you are declaring is that if I depart Tsinia, my kinsmen will die?"

"'Tis so," Athron answered.

"Then it is how I feared it would be. Kovon is a deadly enemy, more so than Darthorn. He hides in the shadows and waits for the precise moment to attack. He holds out a hand of friendship, believing I will return to Earth if all appears well. Only then will he strike. I am the only one who can defeat him, and Kovon is aware of this. Am I to presume, good Athron, that the swan represents your princess and the feathers her kinsmen?"

"With certainty, my lady."

"Very well. You are all witness to the Oracle, and it will be received earnestly. I will not depart until I have dealt with Kovon." She glared at the speechless council. "Nay spare me your repent, for I am not in the disposition to pay attention to it. You will, nonetheless, bring about what I order. Dispatch word to Kovon that Thya refuses his request to meet. Let it be declared I will not be withdrawing from Tsinia. I am convinced this information will distress him."

She took Alkazar's hand and left the Escos without another word.

⚬

"Still, she defies me!" Kovon roared. "While she breathes, she provides hope to those feeble Tsinians.

Without her, I would retain control of the Changlins and of them. Declare to me, Jakar, what is their thought of their princess? How do they react to her stubborn temperament?"

"'Tis sad, my lord. They are blinded from the truth. She is pathetic. She has refused to acknowledge the crown, yet they shut their eyes, convinced that she is their redeemer. The fools exist by the Oracles; it matters not what they observe with sight. After our beloved Darthorn conjured and caused destruction to her land, she still declined to aid her kinsmen. They continue to retain hope as most believe their future is predetermined. They fear you not, my lord."

"Is that so?" Kovon said. "Then I will bestow upon them a reminder that Senx finally has a warlord who will instill fear into their hearts."

Jakar kept silent, though he thought of a few comments he considered wise to keep to himself.

"Yet you compose error in your judgement of Thya," Kovon continued, "for she is a powerful Ganty and possesses a gift. My father related this ahead of his decision to conclude his being." Jakar squirmed at Kovon's words. "She is undeniably a powerful Tsinian. A worthy enemy, one that ought not to be thought of lightly."

"Indeed," said Jakar.

"It matters not. She will be of little consequence. As she has refused to comply with my demands. I will eradicate their princess and entrust the deed in your capable hands."

Jakar bowed. "Very good, my lord."

Kovon pulled a small, ornamental bottle from beneath his kimono.

"Let this liquid flow into Thya's chalice," Kovon instructed. "The poison will react immediately when she swallows it. It matters not how little, for the potion is lethal. Naught of Valcan's skill could aid her. Within moments, she will cease to exist, and I will have removed Tsinian's saviour. Thereafter, I will obtain my reward, as will you."

"I am eager to serve and satisfy my new master. It will be done." Jakar turned to leave.

"Jakar," Kovon called out, "do not fail me."

"My lord, I will surrender my existence to your cause."

"And so, you will – if you fail." Kovon dismissed him. Why did his father amuse himself with the Tsinians for so long? He was a pathetic fool.

Kovon had always considered his father to be a fierce warlord who was feared by all, but now he knew different. There was no order within the city, and even though the Senxs were loyal, they showed a lack of respect for their new lord. Kovon remedied this almost immediately. What did the loss of a few lives matter to him? It was a small price to pay for respect.

Within weeks, their food supply was rationed, as it was more important that produce was sold rather than eaten. Kovon needed allies outside of Senx if his plan for domination were to succeed; he needed contact with the Outlanders. His villagers had barely enough food for themselves and could not afford another mouth to feed, so breeding stopped, which was Kovon's intent.

Senxs were publicly flogged if they grumbled about the terrible conditions. If any dared to break the warlord's command, they were tortured into obedience or died under the effort.

Able Senxs were trained with weapons, thus increasing Kovon's army, though half of them would have turned and ran at the sight of battle.

Within a month, Kovon was finally satisfied he had the respect he demanded from his kinsmen. His plan was in motion, and he relished the thought of the Tsinians on their knees.

Both Kezar and Thya curled up on the sofa, chatting and giggling and enjoying one another's company. It was getting late in the afternoon when the conversation took on a serious note.

"I do not feel tis prudent to disregard Kovon's hand of friendship," Kezar declared.

"Ought I to progress when he summons then?"

"With the death of Darthorn, we exist in the belief that the threat has elapsed. That we retain peace."

"Why do you imagine this?" Thya asked.

"Kovon has not displayed a regard of desire to control Tsinia. Why fear him? Where are the signs of want? He is not similar to Darthorn. He has not raised his hand against us, and I believe tis prudent to accept his attempt at peace. I request pardon if I remark out of turn."

"Nonsense, Kezar. Tis good you voice your thoughts, though you are mistaken. Have you forgotten tis remarked that the hand of Kovon slew our rulers? I have encountered him, and I have sighted for myself the evil in his heart. I am convinced you have more to fear than ever. It frightens me to realise your thoughts. Certainly, we retain peace at this moment. Yet for what duration? Believe me, Kezar, the battle is just commencing."

"If that is so, then tis prudent to grasp the hand that Kovon extends."

Thya did not want to continue this discussion and so conceded. "Possibly I was rash in my judgement. I will allow more reflection."

"Many have not sighted Kovon, and I am one. I only gather information about him in passing. I desire to become familiar, Thya. How does he sight?" Kezar asked bashfully.

"With what you have perceived, how do you envision him?" Thya teased.

Kezar thought hard for a moment. "I vision a handsome Senx. Black hair similar to his father, young, almost representative of coming of age. I sight him gentle and obedient to his peers."

Thya laughed. "He is indeed handsome, though his eyes are cold. I am doubtful of his obedience. I believe he respects not one, other than himself. As for sighting young, in youth he does, though his face reveals signs of a bitter existence. However, he does retain a delicious smile. I believe he has no dilemmas when it comes to companionship."

They blushed and then collapsed into a fit of giggles.

Jakar stood nearby, unseen. He smiled to himself at the thought of telling Kovon what he had just heard. It seemed disappointing to harm a Bora, especially one as beautiful as Thya. Jakar was certain she would have satisfied Kovon, and it now looked as though she was changing her mind. She might even call upon him. Even so, orders were orders, and he wanted to satisfy his new master.

Neither woman saw the bottle. They were far too busy laughing to notice the green liquid being poured into the wine pitcher.

Kezar was more to Jakar's taste, young and innocent. Perhaps Kovon would award her to him after he gained control of Tsinia. It would be a shame to vision her beauty in chains. Jakar was certain Kovon would not decline a small request from a loyal servant.

Before long, Thya stood up and walked over to the

pitcher. Jakar watched in anticipation as she poured herself a chalice of wine. Words were exchanged, and then, to his horror, Kezar took it from her and drank the wine with relish. Within seconds, the cup fell from Kezar's hand. She grabbed at her throat, her eyes widening in horror. The last thing Jakar saw before he fled was Thya catching Kezar's dead body.

Her screams rang through the Recas and beyond. The frightened servants rushed into the attendance room to see Thya cradling Kezar.

"Summon for Valcan!" she screamed. Only there was no need. Thya had alerted most of the city, and Valcan was soon by her side.

"Kezar is beyond my aid," he announced.

"What? Can you not deliver her back to me?" Thya cried. "What requirement is your gift?"

"Her breath was forfeited ahead of my arrival. I cannot recover a soul."

Thya bowed her head.

Omad and Alkazar arrived, shocked by the sight. Alkazar ran to Thya's side and held her while she wept.

"What has occurred?" Omad asked.

"We were enjoying each other's company when she collapsed." Thya sobbed.

"For what reason did this occur?" Omad questioned. "Kezar was healthy, was she not?" He looked to Valcan for confirmation.

"'Tis not a natural death," he said.

"The wine!" Thya jumped to her feet. "She consumed the wine before she collapsed."

Valcan looked for the cup, which he found a short distance from Kezar's body. He sniffed it, and his expression turned solemn. "Tis what I feared – scrikler."

"Scrikler? What is that?" Thya wiped her eyes.

"Tis a rare poison originating from the Outlands," Valcan answered. "Whoever poisoned the wine went to great efforts in the creation of this potion."

"It was I who ought to have consumed the wine," Thya explained. "I poured it, only Kezar seized it from me. Tis I who ought to be lying dead."

"Nay, it is not," Omad announced sternly. "Kezar sacrificed her existence for the sake of yours. Alkazar, protect our lady well, for I fear there is a traitor in our midst. My lady, you are not to eat or drink anything unless I permit it. Do you understand?"

"I will not allow a fellow Tsinian to taste my food prior to myself."

"Nay, my lady, nor I," Valcan agreed. "I am acquainted with the scent of poison. If your refreshments have been tampered with, I will hold awareness. Depart with Alkazar and remain in the Tora until my return. I deem you require my aid."

Alkazar escorted Thya away from the room.

In the past, Alkazar had taught Thya how to meditate, and by the time Valcan returned to the Tora, he was surprised to find Thya well and coherent. Thya talked openly about her fears.

"If I had only approved the encounter with Kovon, naught would have occurred. Tis I who caused the death of my friend."

"Nay, my lady," Valcan objected. "Tis prudent that you did not venture to Senx, for I am secure in my thoughts that you would not be present."

"Why did the council not heed our lady's concerns?" Alkazar asked him. "If they had treated your belief earnestly, we would have been more aware. They could have prevented Kezar's death."

"I disagree with you both," Valcan protested. "There is naught to place blame onto, other than Kovon."

Silence followed. Alkazar was then asked to leave so Thya could rest. She finally settled down to sleep but was troubled by the thought of what light would bring.

The Secret Watcher

THE SACRED CHANGLINS WERE CARRIED out of the Plecky towards the funeral pyre. Thya, believing it was her duty to do so, carried the first of the stones. Omad was next in line, then Nimas, Zarc, and finally Valcan. All five bearers wore white, as was the tradition. Kezar's body was anointed, dressed, and shrouded in gold-coloured cloth. It was a solemn day for all.

Thya was led to her place and asked by Omad to speak to her fellow Tsinians. Even though she was nervous at the thought of addressing her kinsmen, she knew what to say, as if she had performed the speech before. A hidden strength filled her being, and she spoke clearly.

"Citizens of Tsinia, although my acquaintance of Kezar is little, I believed her to be a tender-hearted

Bora with a caring nature. A Tsinian who will be sadly missed. As we mourn, let us not fail to remember the existence she has redeemed by the surrender of her own. For that, I will be forever indebted, as will you all. She has bestowed upon us an opportunity to continue in our struggles and to fight against the darkness closing upon us. Kezar will be missed as my confidante and friend. I will demonstrate to you all that her death will not be in vain. Heed me, my kinsmen. In the presence of you all, I voice my oath: I will perform all that is in my power to prevent Kovon from dominating Tsinia. I will defend my nation and my kinsmen. Although the foreboding of warfare is ever greater, retain the courage yourselves; together we will preserve our history and our future. Praise to the Changlins."

Many wanted to cheer their princess yet remained silent. A dark cloud had lifted, their hearts lightened by her words. At last, she had acknowledged their fight was her own.

Instead of the sombre death march that was sung with the lighting of the pyre, the villagers rejoiced, singing a song which Thya was led to believe was older than the first written Oracle. It celebrated Tsinia and all who lived within her boundaries.

During her speech, Thya felt strong and independent, but though her heart lightened with the joyful chorus, her soul carried a burden so heavy she could barely lift her head.

"Valcan," she called.

On hearing his name, he immediately appeared by her side. "My lady."

"I am weary. Is it permitted to depart?"

"With certainty. I will escort you myself."

Amid the eyes of her citizens, Valcan and Thya drifted away from the crackling wood.

Alkazar was anxious to know why Thya had departed and, on hearing her speech, how she expected to defeat the new warlord. He attempted to follow, only Siren held him back.

"Why do you pursue her? She has not summoned for your counsel," Siren said.

"Our lady requires conversation; she retains a heavy heart. I believe she has requirement of me. I will progress."

"'Tis not an obligation, Alkazar," Siren lectured. "'Tis not your concern, and I will be shamed if you withdraw. I am your betrothed, and our wedlock is to be entered upon presently. You ought to be by my side, console my grief."

Alkazar's temper flared, and he grabbed Siren's arm and pulled her away from prying eyes.

"Thya is your princess and the rightful heir to Tsinia, yet you are without honour and respect for her standing. She demands her subjects to be loyal and support her in these dark moments, yet you dig your sharpened claws in whenever her back is turned. For this, I am ashamed to name you as my betrothed.

Your spiteful resentment has dismantled what remained of my love for you, and I am doubtful it will ever return."

Siren slapped his face. "Pursue her then! You warrant one another. I understood from the first sight of my princess that she would attain your affection. So, proceed, only be aware you have created an enemy out of the generation of Humal presently and forever more."

She glared at him before stomping away. Alkazar watched her leave. He felt no pity, no remorse. In fact, for the first time since his betrothal to Siren, he felt free. The chains that had dragged him down, slowly choking the life out of him, had finally broken. He left in haste to the Recas.

"That was well done, my lady," Valcan said. "You have dispersed the gloom that hovered above us. We rejoice in your decision; although, I did not doubt your loyalty."

She did not answer.

Valcan saw she was settled. "Rest, my lady. I will call upon you presently."

"Summon Alkazar to my council."

"'Tis not required," Alkazar said as he entered the room.

Valcan left, closing the door quietly behind him.

"Oh, Alkazar, what would I do without you? Come, sit." She motioned to an empty seat beside her. "You understand me well. Is there naught I can conceal from you?"

"'Tis not accurate, Thya. There is much you can instruct me on, much to be learnt. You are wise beyond your years. Shortly, you will disregard your past."

Thya sat up. "Never," she snapped. "You mistake me. I have bequeathed a vow that will aid my kinsmen, and I intend to retain this. However, once peace has resumed, I will depart. I possess a home in a faraway place, and unless you have been there and sighted it for yourself, you could never understand why I choose to return."

"You are accurate. I cannot understand why you would desire to exist in a world filled with destruction and intent to destroy one another. You are a similar species. Why do you remove breath so unnecessarily?"

"How can you remark this when your planet behaves identically? You have studied my land from books, not reality. How can you fathom? You do not retain awareness of the beauty that lays there, the love and kindness and hope." A tear rolled down her cheek.

"If only you had such passion for your own domain. Instruct me, Thya, and force me to understand." He raised her chin and gazed into her eyes. "If I kiss you, I will be punished for tis against the code to touch a Ganty with the intent of desire. Yet if I am thrown unclothed into Death Valley, it would be worth it for this."

Alkazar bent his head and kissed her softly on her lips, an act he had been desperate to fulfil since their first meeting. To his relief, she did not fight off his advances. He could feel her desire and sensed she ached for him as much as he ached for her. He could not hold himself back any longer, and the fever of his passion rained upon her lips. His kiss deepened; the urgency grew. He felt her quiver in his arms and knew she was as desperate for this physical interaction as he was. But then she froze and pulled away from him with a pained expression.

"We will cease this." She pushed Alkazar away. "The Changlins summon me, and I must withdraw. You, my love, will return to your betrothed, for tis there you belong, not with me."

Thya turned to leave, only Alkazar took hold of her arm. "I am betrothed not, though I fear we have gained a foe, one we ought to be wary of."

Thya turned to face him. "By the code, you cannot withdraw from your contract."

"That is so. However, I did not. Tis Siren who released me. She is aware, as are others, of my love for you."

"I am saddened by her loss, though not for yours.

From the introduction of Siren, I retained uncertainty of your match. Then you are unrestrained?"

He nodded. "That is so."

"Then you will accompany me to the Plecky. We will discourse with the Changlins together, for only they can consent to our union."

By the will and order of the sacred stones, Thya and Alkazar consummated their love in the Plecky. Alkazar cradled Thya in his arms, gazing in wonder at the sacred stones and at the light burning within.

"I am familiar with the connection you retain with the Changlins, except I currently sight for myself the unique gift you possess."

Thya laughed. "You all hold a connection with the Changlins. They were aware of our intent prior to the revealment of our feelings. They sense the hearts of Tsinians. You remark as though the Changlins have not communicated with Ganties before."

"They have not."

She sat up, surprised. "So, my mother did not possess the ability to perceive their voices?"

"She did not."

"Then why me, Alkazar? Why am I so unique?"

"Such queries cannot be replied to. However, I retain belief in the Oracles. Your destiny is to aid your kinsmen, and you possess a power within you that can do just that. Do not regard this as a burden, Thya. You have been provided with a gift unlike any other. Though tis not understood how significant or the length the power may reach, employ it wisely and master it. I will be by your side as you undertake this deed." They embraced, only it was cut short by a frantic calling of Thya's name.

"That surely was not the Changlins, for I, too, perceived it." Alkazar chuckled.

"It sounded like Salco," she said. "Come, dress. I sense the urgency in his tone."

Hand in hand, they left in search of Salco, finding him walking towards the Tora, calling Thya's name in desperation.

"Salco!" Alkazar shouted to gain his attention. "Why do you bellow your lady's name as though she is a creature of the woods? State, what is the haste?"

"Oh, Alkazar, praise to the Changlins that I encountered you both, for I have searched far and wide." He stopped to catch his breath. "Alkazar, you are requested by the esteemed council to proceed at once to the Escos. You, my lady, were not summoned, though I feel tis my duty to escort you also and to convey to you both the findings."

"What is there to report, Salco? We will depart immediately."

"A trial is to be entered upon."

"A trial! What trial?" Alkazar questioned.

"Salco, enlighten me. What has occurred in my land?" Thya commanded.

"We have apprehended an informer," Salco explained.

"A spy? In Tsinia? This cannot be. Tis grave revelation indeed that one of our own would betray us. Name the traitor," Alkazar demanded.

"You are misled, Alkazar. The informer is not of Tsinia. Tis a Senx."

Thya gasped. "A Senx in Tsinia? Are you confident of this?"

Salco did not answer. They walked into the Escos to find the council seated and in mid-discussion. Zarc stood up as they entered.

"My lady," he sputtered. "Your presence is not required. Only Alkazar has been called upon to attend."

"Tis not my right to be present?" she asked.

"The council has ruled since the passing of our sovereigns, and we will continue to do so until the monarchy is restored. Do you desire to bear the crown as is your right?" Zarc smiled smugly, knowing well what her answer would be.

"You are aware of the position I hold on this," Thya retorted. "However, as you demand so much from me, I expect to be included with resolves that are formed with concern of Tsinia from the hereafter. Is that understood?"

Zarc sat back down without comment.

Omad rose from his seat. "I would not permit an alternative, my lady." He bowed then re-seated.

"Excellent. Then let us resume," she said.

Alkazar took Thya's arm and led her to the thrones situated opposite the council's semicircle.

Tasark stood up. "Darthorn always seemed to know our counterattacks, and we have for some while suspected an informer. Until Kezar's death, we did not retain suspicion that one of our own would betray us. Yet if the spy was to be a Senx, how was he not sighted? The conclusion was revealed in an Oracle.

"Little is recognised of our foe. If we had known they possessed gifts of their own, we would have tightened our security and become increasingly vigilant. Despite this, a snare was arranged to capture the warlord's messenger, which, by the grace of the Changlins, we were capable of achieving. Now, to the present. The esteemed council has convened to judge and lay sentence upon the informer."

His speech finished, and he took his seat as Omad rose.

"Well voiced, Tasark. On to the explanation of why our loyal friend Alkazar is present." He signalled for Alkazar to step forward. "As you will presently sight, our captive is endowed with a gift that you, Alkazar, are acquainted with. He has declined our demands for compliance, and tis hoped your talents could be employed."

Alkazar, although puzzled, bowed and said, "I am at your service as always."

Thya, too, was puzzled. "Bring the prisoner forth."

Alkazar and Thya gasped. Two guards dragge

something towards them, only all they could see was a pair of shackles clattering forwards as if walking by themselves. However, the strangest sight was the smaller-sized shackles suspended in mid-air. A ghost was Thya's first thought. Alkazar laughed aloud, making the council jump.

"I understand why I was brought forth," he said. "Though I am well acquainted with this gift, I am sad to remark I do not retain the power to cancel the enchantment. My talents lie only in the tuition of such gifts, not the removal. I am unable to aid you, though I believe there is one among us who can."

Thya listened to Alkazar, only her mind wandered back to the dreadful afternoon when she and Kezar laughed and enjoyed each other's company. She visualised Kezar raising the poisoned cup to her lips.

She snapped out of her memory, and Thya pointed a finger at the chained prisoner. "You murdered Kezar. Tis you who deposited scrikler into the wine." There was a stunned silence as she walked towards the unseeable figure. "I command you to reveal yourself." She lifted her arms and spread her fingers wide. "I, heir of Tsinia, guardian of the Changlins, command you to unveil yourself."

As if her words were a spell, a scared, pathetic-looking Senx clad in worn trousers and a soiled jacket was revealed. Thya lowered her hands to her side, her sight still upon the spy.

"Your name?" she commanded.

"Jakar," he spluttered.

Alkazar watched on with pride as the council gazed in wonder.

"You have been detained for slaying and for being a herald to our enemy. In advance of your judgement, remark to me, who issued the order to poison the wine?"

Omad was slightly stunned by her question. Jakar was not. He stood as straight as his bent body would allow, lifted his head, and answered, "My lord and master, Kovon, the great warlord of Senx."

"And declare, what will transpire when he discerns of your failure?"

With that, Jakar turned back into the quivering, helpless Senx he was before.

"You have responded to my query. Remove him," she commanded.

The guards came forwards to escort the messenger away.

"Safeguard his wellbeing and treat him justly," she added.

Thya did not return to the throne but walked to the addressing star. She faced the council, who were too stunned to speak and sat open-mouthed.

"As you have witnessed, Jakar is not responsible for Kezar's death, nor of being an informer."

The council was silent no more.

"Not responsible?" they protested.

"My friends, permit the lady to speak," Alkazar said.

Once the noise quieted down, Thya continued. "He was heeding orders from his lord, as you have done yourselves when you were governed. Kovon is the enemy. Tis he who is blamed and he who will be punished, not his herald."

"You would absolve this informant and permit him release to prolong his surveillance?" Zarc quizzed.

"Certainly not. He will return to Senx without his ability. I hold the belief he will not hinder us again."

A member of the council who had so far been silent spoke out. "How do you propose to eliminate his ability? You are not a sorceress. Though we have witnessed a metamorphosis in your persona that astounds us, we are doubtful you can expel such a possession. Only the Changlins can execute such a feat, as you are familiar with, Alkazar."

Alkazar's face reddened. "You fools!" he growled. "Are you blind? Did you not sight the impossible? The informer cannot retain his gift. Did you not sight the wonder our lady performed? Was it not her power and hers alone that uncloaked our enemy? I have accompanied the princess to the Plecky. I have beheld the parallel between the Changlins and herself, and I am convinced. Tis not the Changlins that supply her with power; tis she who powers the Changlins."

There was an almighty uproar. His statement shocked even Thya. Alkazar ignored the shouts and cries, and he raised his voice above the others. "Have you not regarded the peace around us since our lady's arrival? Omad, you yourself expressed alteration in our sacred stones. When it was uncertain if she would retain breath while in the proximity of death, the light within faded. And when she revived, so did the light."

"Tis so, Alkazar," Omad confirmed. "Nevertheless, what you remark is close to impossible. The Changlins have been the source of Tsinia's power ahead of our lady's arrival. The stones have guided and provided us with the elements to survive. If what you remark has any genuineness, then how have we succeeded to exist?"

The others agreed, but Alkazar was ready with his reply. "We have existed, my loyal friends, because Thya existed. In a different dimension from us was she active, and for this reason, so were the Changlins."

Tasark stood. "Then what transpired prior to her birth? Enlighten me to this?"

"Have the Oracles not foretold a Tsinian born with the capability and gifts unlike another? The Changlins held awareness of her pending arrival. Though merely a myth discoursed in passing, you currently sight before you a legend."

Again, they argued among themselves until Omad silenced them.

"Are you confident of this? If what you remark is genuine, I rejoice and praise the Changlins and bestow worship to our lady. Reveal to us, at once. How can you be free from doubt?"

Thya felt she had been silent long enough. "Though I am still acquiring awareness about who and what I am, and I'm not as yet sure how much ability I possess, I am aware I retain the gift of Flite, bestowed to all Ganties. In addition to this, I possess the gift of Yepsy."

Everyone was silent, except a sudden intake of breath among the council. Thya continued, "I sensed a connection with the Changlins the moment I stepped foot in Tsinia and am led to gather that I am the only Ganty who retains this attachment. Although I do not agree nor disagree with Alkazar's certainty, I feel an inner strength, which I am continuing to master. I hope that my power, depending on how much I retain, will aid Tsinia in the fight against Kovon."

Omad turned and addressed Alkazar. "You are witness to these wonders?"

"I am. We came upon the gift by chance, though tis written about. I have tutored and trained our lady on the employment of Yepsy. I believe there is naught among you who are ignorant of the code." No one answered, so he continued. "Our lady holds the ability to control the forces of nature, which leads me to believe she has a connection with the Changlins. This alone is remarkable, yet what we have just witnessed leaves me complexed. I am uncertain what further abilities she may possess; we are continuing in our understanding." He turned and smiled at her. "What I do believe is that her arrival was a blessing. Even though I am unsure how she will conquer Kovon, I am convinced she will."

Alkazar walked to Thya and kneeled before her.

"Thya, heir of Tsinia and guardian of the Changlins, I pledge to you my trust, love, and service until my final breath."

Thya felt deeply moved by his words. "And I accept your service and will hold you to your oath, Alkazar."

All of the councillors stood, bowed, and swore an oath to protect their princess.

Once the pledges were over, they re-seated. They felt the change. Even though she had yet to accept the crown, many believed they once again had a ruler. The council waited eagerly for her command, and Thya sensed a respect and power of authority. She returned to the throne before addressing the council. "Tis the period of alteration. I will face my destiny and accept my fate, whatever that is. I shall compete in battle if the requirement arises. I believe Alkazar is of the same mind. I retain comprehension of the code and of the arts, and I doubt there is more to ascertain. We will release Jakar from his chains and return him to his land with a declaration for the great warlord. I will encounter with him in one tril moon."

Omad rose from his seat to speak. "Though we desired an alliance, tis obvious now that will not occur, and we beg absolution for our demands on you. They were unjust. We are but a peaceful race and consider defence only for the protection of our land. Even so, you have sighted that we do not retain weapons and employ our powers only as a deterrent, which themselves are few.

"We have so far protected Tsinia, though I fear the warlord's power is growing, and I am doubtful we can resist longer."

"Be seated, Omad," Thya instructed. "You are not required to stand to address me. I do not desire warfare. I hope my encounter with Kovon will conclude the evil shadowing my kinsmen."

Omad re-seated and continued his questioning. "If not war, then let it be voiced how you purpose to halt the warlord when he retains the power of the Darkeye?"

"I will destroy the Darkeye," Thya declared.

"Surely, you do not presume to venture to Senx unassisted?" Tasark asked.

"With certainty, I believe Kovon would desire this approach."

"Are you not fearful he will prepare a trap for you, my lady?" Tasark retorted.

"Do not be troubled. I will spin my own snare."

"Though I do not take pleasure in uttering these words, I believe I ought to," Tasark pressed. Thya nodded in acceptance. "What if you do not succeed, my lady? What will befall us? If Alkazar is just and your resource powers the Changlins, then all will be lost and Tsinia will be destroyed."

Alkazar broke in. "And if our lady does not face Kovon and we position an attack, we again become defeated and our land will be seized. These are dark moments, my friends, yet I sight a light that glows brighter."

"What if you fail?" Tasark mumbled.

"I will not," she said. "Although I understand your fear. Organise provisions, Omad, and have your kin prepared to depart at a moment's notice if this satisfies you."

Tasark nodded.

"Tis late and I have much to undertake. Return Jakar to me," she commanded.

Within moments, the two guards brought Jakar in and forced him to kneel before her. His head remained bent, too frightened to look at her.

"Jakar, messenger and servant to Kovon of Senx, I choose to be merciful and spare your miserable existence." He lifted his head with surprise as a guard unclasped his chains.

"Let not one voice that Thya is unjust or unruly. Depart and relate to your master that I desire to convene with him in one tril moon from the present."

Jakar smiled. The message would please Kovon and should ease his punishment for failure.

"And be aware," she continued, "if you are caught

upon my land thereafter, you will sustain pain for your defiance."

Jakar eyed Thya suspiciously before getting up and running out of the Escos.

Although Jakar returned with good news, he was severely punished for failing to kill Thya and getting caught. Kovon considered his options.

Jakar was inadequate. He couldn't complete an effortless order without messing it up. Only, some good had come of it. Thya intended to come to Senx. Once she was upon his land, he would tend to her. This time, though, she would not depart.

Kovon couldn't decide whether to retain and employ her at his leisure or eliminate her once she had moaned with both pleasure and pain. He called for an attendant.

"Ready a chamber for confinement. I am anticipating a guest." He smiled smugly.

Final Conflict

THYA RETURNED HER ATTENTION TO THE council. "I understand you have many queries for me. Nevertheless, I am tired and will rest. Alkazar, you will escort me to the Plecky, and I will then return to the Recas where I require council from Alkazar, Omad, and Pertius."

Thya stepped down from the throne, took Alkazar's arm, and left the Escos.

"I appreciate your words, Alkazar. I know who I am and where my duty lies. My burden has lifted since I accepted my responsibilities. Defeating Kovon represents an itch that requires scratching, naught more than that."

He nodded. "'Tis not until I voiced my findings that I finally understood. 'Tis a huge liberation for me as the conclusion plagued me for some while. We are both granted peace."

They reached the Plecky, only Alkazar would not enter.

"'Tis not a concern of mine, Thya. I will remain until your reappearance."

When Thya emerged from the Plecky, she felt stronger and more determined than ever.

Thya was lost to her thoughts and did not speak until they reached the Recas.

"Alkazar, I desire for you to be aware of how significant your companionship is. I could not have reached this juncture if it was not for you."

He bowed and motioned for her to enter before following quietly behind.

Pertius and Omad rose from their seats as Thya entered the attendance room. She bade them to remain seated and sat in deep thought before speaking.

"I do not know what will occur in Senx, so I am unable to prepare myself. Regardless, I am certain that with my powers and by the will of the Changlins I will defeat Kovon. Tsinia will once again exist in peace.

"What has been revealed to me, and what I knew in my heart, is that I am compelled to destroy the Darkeye. Alas, I am unacquainted with this power. Omad, how informed are you?"

"Little, I fear, my lady," he answered. "Though tis

understood to be a crystal, large and black as its heart."

"Alkazar, perhaps you retain an understanding of the Eye, for it seems more of your concern," Thya said.

"I am of some understanding," he replied. "The Darkeye is held within Darthorn's dwelling – pardon, Kovon's dwelling. Though tis not acknowledged in what location. The Lords of Senx employ the Eye for guidance to sight future occurrences."

"As do we with the Oracles," Thya said.

"Tis so," Alkazar answered. "Only, the Darkeye holds an evil strength within it, familiar to us as the Dark Force. The Lord of Senx controls the employment of this force, and we have all witnessed its strength."

"Tis why it ought to be destroyed," Thya declared.

"With certainty, my lady," Alkazar agreed. "Yet, how do you intend to achieve this feat?"

"I am undecided as yet. Even so, I am not anxious. I believe that when the moment arises, I will understand what must be done."

Omad nodded. Thya knew she needed to give the impression of having the demeanour of one without a care, positive and brave. She hoped they would not acknowledge a pretence. Could it be possible that Alkazar was just in his conclusion? Will the Changlins provide me with the strength I need? Even though I act as though I obtain courage, I'm still uncertain what strength I truly hold.

Thya laughed joyfully as she chatted with Pertius and Alkazar, as though she had nothing to fear.

"Advise me, Pertius, with awareness of my intentions, is there a section of the code that forbids me to proceed?"

"Nay, my lady. Not to my recollection. An act of war relaxes the code somewhat. If I remember otherwise, you will be the first I inform."

"'Tis good," Thya said. "Omad, I am told that unless I accept the crown, you retain the title of governor. Therefore, I require your consent to proceed to Senx alone. Is it permitted?"

"'Tis, my lady, yet I believe you would proceed regardless."

Thya laughed but noticed the others did not feel it was right to be merry at such a climatic time.

She held her hands out. "My loyal friends, your fight is verging to a conclusion. Why so glum? Begin the celebrations. Rejoice in your freedom," she declared.

"How are you convinced you will be victorious when you understand not what will occur or how you are to defeat Kovon?" Pertius asked.

Thya looked to Alkazar for an answer.

"If the guardian of the Changlins assures all will be well, then it will be so. Do not query her judgement," Alkazar lectured.

Thya smiled. "Well remarked."

"And yet," he continued, "we ought to prepare for an assault. Omad, I believe tis prudent to be organised."

"Agreed."

There was a strained silence. "Very well," she relented. "Do as you will. Now, allow me my rest, and do not disturb me for I will be in vigil from first light until my departure. Omad, prepare my escort; I depart as soon as the tril moon is upon us."

All three stood to leave.

"Alkazar, linger a while," she called. He re-seated while the others took their leave.

"I hold preference to pass my moments with you rather than in solitude. Alas, the Changlins command this, so remain a while and bestow companionship and love."

She held her arms out to him, and he picked her up, carrying her out of the attendance room and into her bedroom amid the astonishment of the servants.

Thya spent the following day in solitude, meditating and relaxing her mind and body to prepare for the confrontation. She decided to give Kovon the impression she was venturing to Senx in the hope of another alliance. There was no reason for him to think otherwise. If he had the smallest inclination to Thya's resolve, he would most likely be prepared for her, but the Changlins assured her he knew nothing of her plan. An element of surprise was the only way she would defeat the warlord. Even so, her mind was split in two, and she had a hard time struggling between doubt and certainty.

How can I feel so calm and be so sure of myself when I have no awareness of what will occur or how to destroy Kovon? Yet, still, I believe I will succeed. Tis the unknown that confuses me.

The time came for her departure, and Alkazar was soon by her side. She dressed in a white, flowing silk dress that symbolised peace, and she wore her mother's necklace. With her hair loose, she looked and felt like a Ganty. This new awareness caused her determination to grow.

"Alkazar, you appear unrested," Thya said. "Did you not sleep well?"

"My rest was troubled by disturbing images. Thya, I implore you. Do not proceed to Senx. I retain a belief you will face unknown dangers."

"Do you not deem me fit to protect myself?"

"You misunderstand. I do not doubt your powers. I am concerned for your safety. I am convinced Kovon holds perilous intentions, and I desire for you to be prepared."

Thya smiled. "I am humbled by your concern; however, I have envisioned this scenario. When his intention is identified it will be dealt with. Fret not."

Alkazar returned her smile. "Thya, I sense a transformation and acceptance within you, and for this, I am grateful. Although, I pity any Bora who comes against you."

Thya laughed. "I am a force to be reckoned with. Only, do not pity Kovon. He warrants punishment."

"And yet you are not aware how you will achieve this?"

Thya didn't answer. Instead, she took his arm and led him from the room. Before opening the main door, he turned to her. "I pray to the Changlins that you succeed and are returned unharmed. I will not exist without you, Thya. Continue in safety, and do not partake of any refreshments offered to you. Remain keen and aware." He embraced her tightly. "Oh, how I hoped it would not arrive at this."

With determination and courage, Thya set out on her journey. Omad was among her escorts and spoke feverishly of his worries. No matter how much assurance she gave them, they grew more concerned about her safety. In the end, Thya gave up and wouldn't answer his questions in the fear of sounding rude.

After completing half the journey, Thya dismissed the escorts against Omad's wishes. She wanted to arrive at the gates of Senx alone.

The sentries were surprised to see her travelling unaccompanied, and one went in search of her escorts. When he returned empty-handed, he shrugged in bewilderment, unable to believe she dared to come alone. The gate opened, and Thya entered the realm of Senx.

Many Senxs were outside their dwellings, busying themselves with their duties, and paid no heed to Thya. They wouldn't dare to involve themselves in their lord's business; the punishment would be severe. They had witnessed the hand of Kovon before and so kept their heads down, appearing disinterested.

Thya was shocked by the differences with the Senxs from the last time she saw them. Their faces were withdrawn and pale, and their garments showed signs of age and wear. How she pitied them. Her Senx escorts were silent as they took her to the chamber where Kovon waited.

She turned and curtsied to the sentries. "I appreciate your pleasant company." The bewildered look on their faces satisfied her.

They opened the door to the great chamber and then left. Thya entered alone.

Kovon was seated in a recliner, looking comfortable and relaxed. It seemed he had rid the chamber of the cheerful gold decor since her last visit. The dull silver now created a dark and sombre ambiance. He stood and acknowledged Thya's appearance with a wide grin.

"Thya, I am delighted by your acceptance to convene with me once more."

"You will address me as 'my lady.' This is my right."

"Then you will address me as Lord Kovon."

"Do not believe I am here by choice," she retorted. "I came in the hope we can arrive at an understanding. Despite this, I ought to eliminate you for the assassination of Kezar and for the fear you and your father have instilled in the hearts of my kinsmen."

"Kezar. An unfortunate accident."

Thya didn't dare speak, so she stared at him until she could control what came out of her mouth.

"At present, you are the Lord of Senx. My kinsmen are under the impression you would agree to an alliance absent from wedlock, though I am doubtful of this. Even so, they have persuaded me to converse with you; although, I believe I am wasting my breath. Since Darthorn's unexpected demise, I sense my kinsmen are under a bigger threat."

"How perceptive of you, my lady, and allow me to state how honoured I am by your presence, for I am sure you retain pressing matters to deal with since taking your rightful place among the Tsinians."

Thya read his expression. The darkness in his eyes revealed his true feelings – that he despised her as much as she did him.

He continued, "Believe me when I remark that my heart lightens at your sight. I desire for us to… turn over a new leaf. I believe that is how you would word it back on your home planet. I would like to become more familiar with you, for I have a feeling about us."

She envisioned his sick fantasies if she were ever

defenceless. He smirked, clearly under the impression the situation was in his control. Thya wanted to laugh out loud at his assumption.

"You play games, Lord Kovon. You have not the intention to work towards peace."

"Again, I congratulate you on your perception," Kovon answered. "Certainly, I requested you under false pretences. Tis a perfect opportunity to dispose of my enemy."

"I am present and unarmed. What are you resolved to do, Lord Kovon? Eliminate me?" Thya laughed. "Do you believe tis so effortless? Numerous have attempted and failed, as will you."

Thya knew she should feel terrified and warned herself against her words. However, an inner strength burned through her body and soul, and she felt strong and invincible.

Kovon stepped towards her. His expression was deadly serious and his voice barely a whisper. "I hold not the intention to destroy you at present. I desire satisfaction."

Thya wished she could wipe away the smirk flickering across his face. "You believe you have it worked out, do you not? If you presume I will plead for mercy, then you are mistaken."

Once more, Thya calmed the anger rising within her as Kovon laughed ruthlessly.

"You will plead, my lady, alas not for mercy. I will fulfil your every whim until you implore me further."

This time, she couldn't keep the laughter inside. "You are under a misapprehension, Lord Kovon. I do not feel desire. You repulse me. You are misled by the notion that you attract the opposite sex. Well, permit me to enlighten you. Female Senxs retain extremely poor taste. I will never consent for you to lay one finger upon me."

Thya assumed by then that Kovon would have stopped smiling. It worried her to see him looking so sure of himself.

"We will shortly observe."

Light-headedness overwhelmed Thya. She tried to shake off the dizziness, only she felt a pressing sensation on her temples. She raised her hands and rubbed hard at the ache. However, it did not cease; it grew.

"I, too, retain powers, Thya. An ability that is rarely passed down the generations of warlords."

He ceased smiling and concentrated. She believed he was looking into the depths of her soul.

"You will desire for me. Your need will ache for me. You will do all I require. My will is presently upon you."

Thya tried to speak. Her mouth opened, only no words came out. She could not move, no matter how hard she tried. It was as if a cold hand pressed onto her back. She watched helplessly as Kovon circled her like she was his prey. She sensed him standing behind her yet could not confront him.

Kovon smiled. He finally had her fully in his control. She was similar to all Boras: puppets awaiting instruction from their master. She was naught, certainly not the prophesied saviour of Tsinia. His hand touched her waist, and he felt her quiver. He had control of her body and soul, and she would do whatever he demanded from her. Oh, how he had waited for this moment. He was going to savour every second, take his time, and burn the memory into his mind so he would always remember his biggest conquest. She was exquisite, and he was eager to uncover her shapely body. He ran his fingers along her side, causing her to sigh with desire. It satisfied him immensely.

Thya hoped the shiver was from fear; however, she knew it to be desire. Why was she allowing herself to be fooled by false emotions? Why was he affecting her this way? He repulsed her, did he not? Alkazar was the only man she desired. Thya felt Kovon's hot breath on her neck. She wasn't as disgusted by it as she wanted to be. She was aroused, and her body ached for more. What was happening?

"You retain a quality about you, princess," he whispered in her ear. "A shadow beyond your beauty.

Tis what I have desired. There is an essence in your spirit. I can sense it."

Although Thya could not answer Kovon, she tried with all her might to break free from his will.

"Do not fight me. Not one can resist my power. I will cause this to be pleasant enough."

Thya's mind screamed, but no words passed her lips. What had he done to her? She felt aroused. She did not desire his touch, yet her body yearned for more. Kovon created false lust, and she felt compelled to fight him. Her existence and soul depended on it.

"Relax," he instructed.

He led her to a corner of the chamber, and even though her will told her not to, she followed. Two huge silk pillows appeared on the floor.

"I sense you have surrendered yourself to a Bora recently," he said. "Did you relish the thrill of your interaction? Tis naught compared to what you will sense when I take you. Permit my spirit to engulf you, Thya. Allow my entrance." He led her by the arm to the bedding. "I will transport you to locations and senses you have yet to reach. I will pleasure you until you cry out."

Kovon ordered Thya to lie down on the floor, which she did without resistance. He smiled as her eyes glassed over, and not once did she turn her face away from his. She waited for his next command.

He tied her wrists to the steel railing decorating the side of the chamber.

Thya was ready to give him whatever he wanted of her to get it over with. It seemed pointless to struggle and fight. She regretted allowing herself to be captured so easily. She tried to take her mind to a place where she could forget what was happening to her, only too many questions raced through her mind and she couldn't relax. How could she have been so stupid to believe she was competition to a powerful warlord? What would her demise be? Would he force her to walk off the balcony as she now guessed he had done to his father? If the great Darthorn couldn't resist him, how could she?

Kovon kissed and licked Thya's throat then lowered his aim.

Why can I not resist him? Is he waiting for me to beg? Is that his goal?

Thya sighed in ecstasy as he lowered the dress from her shoulder and kissed her naked skin. It felt right, good even. She wanted more, just like he said she would.

"You sense it, do you not? I am aware of your need. Permit the feeling to flow through you. I sense the fever rising within. The flame of your concealed lust is igniting the core of your essence. Open yourself to me."

"Oh, my lord," she cried as his hands lowered and pressed into her desire.

Oh, how I want him. How I burn for his touch. Why did I ever resist him? He is everything I want. No! What am I thinking? These are not my feelings. He has control of me. His force is creating this false desire.

She knew her true feelings. If she could retain that truth, then perhaps she could fight him.

Two powers fought within her: her own will and that of Kovon's. For a moment, both were in perfect balance.

"Do not fight me, Thya, or this will become unpleasant."

His words were like ice water, cooling her false sense of desire. Alkazar's voice rang through her mind. 'Relax. Empty your thoughts and concentrate solely on what you demand.'

Her mind calmed and cleared, and with it, she rid Kovon's thoughts from her head.

"Nay!" he yelled. "This cannot be. I hold higher power." Only already his will was fading.

Engaging in an inner struggle, Thya broke Kovon's power.

He stood. His fists clenched so tight they turned white. Sweat dripped down his face, and his eyes screwed shut. He willed his power onto her with as much force as he could. However, Thya was suddenly stronger than him.

It wasn't until Thya was certain he no longer had control over her that she felt a burning deep inside.

Not unpleasant, soothing. Energy emerged, giving her strength, a sense of the hidden force. She willed the ties to loosen, visibly un-knotting them.

He had lost the struggle and having used all his power and strength in the battle of minds, he collapsed to the floor. Astonished by her strength, he watched Thya stand. She stared at him; her eyes white. It was as if the light shone through them, and they bore into him. The brightness increased until he could bear it no longer. He turned his face away, but only for a moment; curiosity won. She came towards him, almost gliding. An invisible wind surrounded her, and her hair flew wildly. Kovon thought she looked like a Gestle, a powerful demon from the underworld.

He held no power over her, and for the first time in his existence, he felt vulnerable. Unable to find the strength to crawl away, he waited until she was upon him.

"You are an evil Bora, Kovon. I will obtain payment for the misery you have inflicted."

She came upon him but stopped. Another voice called through her mind. *No. This is not the means. I do not want revenge.*

No sooner had she thought this did the desire for vengeance fade and the fever in her blood subside.

The Darkeye was responsible for the evil shadowing her land. She was certain that without it,

Kovon would be a powerless, humble Senx and no threat to her kinsmen.

"I am compelled to destroy the Darkeye."

"Destroy the Darkeye?" Kovon laughed. "Do you assume tis so effortless? Only a warlord may gaze upon its light."

For a moment, it seemed a problem until a thought entered her mind.

She stretched her arms and willed the Darkeye to appear. Nothing happened, and Kovon laughed.

Thya was not aware if she retained the ability to create things to appear on command; however, she could control nature with the gift of Yepsy. With that thought in mind, she cleared her throat and called out, "Oh, majestic wind of the north, by the grace of the Changlins, I summon you to present yourself."

To Kovon's disbelief, a wind blew around him. It gathered itself until a funnel of air faced Thya. Within moments of the tornado appearing, it had grown. Without voice, Thya commanded the fierce wind to seek the Darkeye and bring it to her. The funnel moved towards the entrance of the chamber, and the brass doors swung inwards, as if an invisible, mighty hand had pushed them open. The tornado disappeared, yet Thya's sight did not leave the doorway. Her attention fixed solely on her command of the wind. She paid no heed to Kovon. He was no threat to her as he lay helpless and silent.

Within moments of the tornado leaving, it

reappeared, bringing a shadow along with it. It wasn't until the funnel was stationary that Kovon realised what was inside.

"Do not undertake what you contemplate," he cried. "I forewarn you, consider what you bring about. You realise not what you possess."

Thya didn't need to deliberate. She knew the Darkeye was the source of Senx's power. The Eye caused the evil that had shadowed Tsinia for far too long. She knew exactly what she was doing.

With a slight movement of her head, the tornado rose from the ground until it could go no further. There it stayed, suspended in mid-air.

In one last effort, Kovon begged her not to destroy the Eye. "Thya, rightful Queen of Tsinia, you are victorious. Retain your motherland, and you will neither perceive nor retain sight of me henceforth. Tis my oath."

At last, Thya heard the words she'd been longing for. Kovon had surrendered.

"Only I implore you, do not destroy the Darkeye."

This, she did not want to hear. If the warlord was willing to conclude his war for the safety of his precious Eye, then certainly it had to be destroyed. She stepped back and let her gaze fall to the ground, and with it, the Darkeye.

The tornado disappeared, and the crystal crashed to the ground. In one last effort, Kovon lunged forward, but it hit the floor with such force it broke into a thousand pieces. The shards littered the chamber, though none lay close to Thya. Many hit Kovon, and he screamed with both pain and sorrow.

Silence followed.

First, he was numb with shock. Then came rage. "You obstinate fool," he spat. "You stupid, unfortunate Bora. You do not comprehend the repercussions of your actions."

He picked himself up from the floor and glared at her. Thya wanted to turn away from the sight of his mangled, bloody face.

"I forewarned," he continued, "though you listen not." He laughed, a maniacal laugh. "With your power and the employment of the Darkeye, you could have ruled the Outlands."

"I do not desire world domination. All I require, all I have ever desired is peace for my kinsmen."

"Tis why I laugh for you, not upon you. The Darkeye would have bestowed the peace you so desperately desire. The Darkeye can be employed for righteousness too. It was my father who displayed a preference for the dark side. You, Thya, you could have commanded all, but tis your loss rather than mine."

Kovon's words did not seem to be said in jest, yet if it was so, then she had indeed made a grave mistake.

They both stared at the broken shards.

"There will be an occasion when you will repent your actions," Kovon warned.

"Possibly. Although, you will not be present to sight the occasion of my regret."

Kovon stood up straight and lifted his head. "So, I receive my judgement. Announce to me, Thya, what is your intent?"

"Tsinians do not condone violence, and I am willing to accept this also. You have suffered enough. You do not retain power and will hurt naught. Without the aid of the Darkeye, you are defenceless. So, Kovon, I allow you to rule Senx as is your right. Though as weak and powerless as you are, tis doubtful your reign will last. I sight unrest among your kinsmen. You will suffer as you attempt to protect your inheritance."

Thya felt she was just.

"You will rue your decision."

"You are naught, Kovon."

With that, she turned her back to him and walked away. Intuition told her she had made a mistake. She turned in time to see him running at her, his hands like claws, wanting to tear her apart. But his strength died suddenly, and he could not continue. His knees buckled, and he fell to the floor defeated.

Once more, Thya felt the mysterious strength burning through her veins. She seemed to grow, becoming tall and menacing. Kovon cowered before her. Her eyes, too, had again changed. They were no longer blue; instead, they glowed white with the same brightness as before. Only this time, he could not look away.

Their eyes locked contact, and his gaze fixed on hers until he could see no more.

"I removed your sight," her ghostly voice echoed through the silent hall. "You will never again sight evil."

Kovon cried, though no tears came. She watched him shake with fear and apprehension.

"Mercy," he cried out. "I beseech you."

A finger touched his quivering lips. The touch, at first gentle, caused a burning sensation. The pain was so intense, so unbearable that he lost consciousness. He awoke moments later as her voice echoed through the darkness.

"I removed your voice. You will never again voice evil."

Kovon lay motionless on the floor unable to see or beg for mercy. He hoped for a quick end to his torment. It was then he heard a distant rumble. The noise expanded until it filled his entire being. Then, without warning, a loud clap of thunder shook Senx and beyond, exploding the chamber's window.

Silence followed, the most frightening sound Kovon had ever heard. He strained to hear the intake of his own breath, only there was nothing. What he heard, or what he thought he heard, would stay with him for the rest of his life. Thya's strange voice echoed, "I removed your hearing. You will never again perceive evil."

Only moments after the end of her wrath, Thya emerged from her trance into reality. She looked wildly around at the devastation. The last thing she remembered was Kovon's attempt to attack her.

Kovon. Where was he?

She found him huddled in the corner looking helpless. The sight sickened her. His eyes were wide in horror. All that could be seen were balls of milky white. His hand reached out to nothing, imploring for help. His mouth opened as if in a scream, only no sound came out. She raised her hands to cover her muffled cry. "'Tis my fault!"

Only, was it her doing? She had no recollection. Something or someone had taken over her mind and body. She felt weak, as though her strength had been zapped from her.

She ran, almost falling, out of the chamber and didn't stop until she was at the gates.

The citizens of Senx ran about in fear. The tremendous thunder had blown out most of their windows, and a strange storm had appeared over the warlord's domain. Although they saw Thya, they paid no heed to her. Even the soldiers were too busy running to aid their master to take notice of one lone female Bora.

Thya struggled to remain conscious, running almost blind through the city. She didn't register where she was or where she was going. She just kept moving down the mountain towards her home until her strength finally failed. Her mouth was parched, and her limbs were so weak she could go no farther. Unable to stay conscious any longer, she collapsed.

Though Thya had instructed that no one accompany her, Alkazar had gathered the gifted Tsinians together, ready to go to battle if their assistance was needed.

Tasark made it his duty to ready the females and ensure essential belongings were packed, just in case they had to leave suddenly.

The citizens of Tsinia were seated upon the ground in prayer when they saw the strange storm appear. Sensing it was not natural, Alkazar stood up in alarm. It was then they heard the almighty thunder and felt the land shake. He believed Thya was in trouble and so called out, "I will not permit our princess to continue alone. Who among you will follow?"

Not one remained seated; all felt it was their duty to aid Thya. Omad nodded to Alkazar.

Although the Tsinians were a peaceful race, if any Senx were to cross their path, there would be trouble. They would take no more. Even Alkazar was bent on getting his hands around Kovon's neck. It never once entered his head that Thya had defeated the warlord. He was certain, as were they all, that Thya had failed and required their help.

I am coming, my love, Alkazar silently called out.

It was on the treacherous mountain path that he spotted her lying across the trail as though dead. With a startled cry, he ran to her. "Thya," he whispered as he turned her over.

She seemed unhurt. In fact, there was not one scratch or mark on her.

On hearing her name, she uttered, though barely a whisper, "Tis done. My kinsmen will exist in peace."

"Praise to our saviour!" Alkazar shouted. "Princess Thya has attained victory over the Lord of Senx."

The cheers echoed through both lands. The Tsinians hugged one another and jumped around with joy. Alkazar carried Thya to Valcan, who waited farther down the trail. The cheers cut off as they waited to hear the healer's proclamation.

Valcan examined Thya, relieved to find her unhurt. "Our princess is thriving. All that is required is rest to recuperate."

The Tsinians rejoiced loudly and continued on,

determined to remove any evil that still lived. Alkazar carried Thya down the mountain while Omad and Valcan silently followed.

There was little resistance from the Senxs. After learning of their warlord's downfall, many of the warriors laid down their arms and bowed their heads in submission. The citizens of Senx celebrated with cheers, tears, and laughter. Some stood still in shock that they were free and able to live as they wanted.

Kovon could not be found. Whether he was aided or walked blindly out of his land, no one knew nor cared.

The Tsinians left Senx without causing any bloodshed.

The Wedding

THYA WAS TAKEN TO THE RECAS WHERE she slept without stirring under the watchful eye of Valcan. Four tril moons passed. When she awoke, she found she had no energy. She couldn't even lift her head. It took a further seven tril moons before Thya could walk unaided.

Alkazar was by her side throughout her recuperation. He was curious about Thya's past life and of the strange world she had been brought up in. He asked her many questions, yet not once did he ask what had occurred in the land of Senx.

A month passed swiftly. Thya at last felt contented. She enjoyed her new life without the threat of death hanging over her and took time explore her beautiful land. She breathed in the sweet atmosphere of Tsinia that was now untainted by the stench of fear.

Her citizens were once again humble and merry, for their hearts were lightened, able at last to live in peace. Thya could not help but be swept away by it all, engulfed by the wonderfully calm existence.

The celebrations continued. So carefree and merry were her kinsmen that she fell in love with them all.

It was at one of the many festivals that the council again offered Thya the crown, believing that this time she would not refuse.

The realisation hit her that if she accepted the title of Queen of Tsinia, she would have to live there permanently and forget her past life. It was a frightening thought.

I know I don't really belong on Earth and that Becky wasn't real, but it's the only life I've known. Can I walk away and accept who I truly am?

Omad instilled the help of a fellow Tsinian so all could hear the presentation. His voice rang out loud and clear. "Thya, Guardian of the Changlins, your nation implores you to once again consider and receive what is rightfully yours. We require a ruler as majestic as yourself to govern our lands. I would gladly renounce my title as head of the council if you were to accept the crown and become the queen you were born to be."

Thya, too, called for the Volume of Voice gift, as she wanted her kinsmen to hear her reply.

"Nay, Omad. I am not prepared to accept the responsibility. I am saddened to announce to you all that tis possible I will never be." Thya paused. "I request that you, Omad, remain as head of the council and govern my land and those who reside in it as you deem fit. I will always remain the princess of Tsinia, and you will forever be in my heart. Nevertheless, I am compelled to remark my farewells. Tis the period of return."

The gathering argued and groaned.

"My loyal subjects, you retain assurance that if I am ever required in Tsinia, on request, I will return. I cherish the period spent among you. Despite that, I don't feel comfortable in Tsinia. It would take much duration for me to think of my land as home. I am content on Earth and miss the life I had there. I trust you will pardon me and come to understand why your princess departed. Do not grieve. Let us celebrate our freedom and permit me the blissful memory of this occasion."

The cheers rang out, and Thya's name was repeatedly chanted. Alkazar, who stood close by, bowed his head. He knew the time would come when she would want to leave. Still, he wasn't prepared for the ache that was upon him. He hoped she would fall in love with Tsinia as well as himself. If only there was more duration. He could not bear to think of a single moment without his beautiful Thya, yet he retained too much dignity to beg her to stay. If she accepted, he would believe it was because of his request alone, and that it would lead to unhappiness. He couldn't permit this sacrifice. If it was her desire to depart, then so be it. He accepted her decision, yet at present, he felt empty, as though she had already withdrawn from his side.

Thya turned to Alkazar. He forced a smile, only she sensed his unhappiness. "Why so glum?" she asked. "You understood that I would eventually depart. I did not present you with promises, Alkazar. You were aware from the start of my intentions, were you not?"

"I understood," he replied. "Even so, I expected you to reconsider."

He looked pleadingly into her face, longing for his words to make a difference.

"Come, consent to a stroll," Thya suggested. "I fear tis too loud to converse, and I desire for you to perceive me well."

Alkazar held out his arm to her, which she took. They made their way through the crowd. The celebrations paused while they passed. Once out of sight, the merriment and dancing continued.

For a while, they walked silently through the woods. Then, not being able to control himself any longer, Alkazar grabbed Thya's waist and pressed her against the trunk of the nearest tree. He made sure no one was around when he planted a kiss on her lips. Once he released her, Thya laughed. They embraced again, this time with less urgency. He tilted her chin and stared longingly into her eyes.

"I love you, Thya, Becky, whoever you are. I cannot

vision an instant without you." He hugged her tightly, afraid to let go.

Thya felt content to stay in his arms forever, only she had something important to ask him and so gently pushed him away.

"Alkazar, I love you with all my heart and soul. Our future has been blessed by the Changlins. You are my soul mate. We are destined to join together, yet you understand how I feel about remaining and I believe you accept my reasons." Alkazar nodded. Thya continued, "There is save one alternative if you would consider it. I would delight in your acceptance of returning to Earth with me."

Thya studied Alkazar's shocked expression.

"I realise tis momentary notice, though I intend to depart in seven tril moons. I sympathise that you may not want to abandon your home and kinsmen. Tis, just I… well, you harbour such interest in my home. I am convinced you would be up for the notion."

"Oh, my sweet Thya," he whispered. He held her face and kissed her gently. "You could not comprehend how blissful I am. Deep down, I yearned you would require me to return with you. Despite that, I would not have mentioned it for fear of rejection."

Thya giggled through her tears. "You will depart with me then?"

"With certainty, if the Changlins permit this," he

answered. "Do not disregard that both our existences are not our own. We are present for a purpose."

Thya took his hands and squeezed them. "They sense our intent and permit this, on the oath we will return if ever called upon. Oh, Alkazar, there is much I long to reveal, much for you to sight and learn. You will relish it there."

She twirled. "I feel so happy I believe I could burst. I desire for everyone to be aware of my joy. My love will return with me!" She suddenly remembered herself. "We are compelled to bestow praise to the Changlins, for tis fitting."

They ran together through the forest, unnoticed by all bar one. Alkazar did not realise that out of silly desire, he had embraced Thya against Siren's tree dwelling.

Siren had not joined in with the celebrations, preferring to share her own company. This was out of shame of her broken betrothal to Alkazar and of her jealousy of Thya. Unfortunately, she had been in residence and had seen and heard all. She would not permit it to transpire. Thya had acquired everything she desired. She was permitted happiness while Siren remained stranded with naught. Nay, Thya would not be victorious on this occasion.

"There will not be a future for you and Alkazar. Tis my curse upon you. You will both experience shame and pain from the loss of a loved one. This I swear upon the name of Humal," she muttered then left her dwelling in search of Valcan.

Thya and Alkazar waited until the next council meeting before speaking of their plans. When Alkazar announced his departure, it was taken calmly, as though it had already been considered. To Thya's relief, the council seemed delighted by the news. Omad spoke of his gladness that she was not returning alone, thankful that someone would be there to protect her. Their only concern was that Tsinia would be left without a tutor of the arts. Neither Alkazar nor Thya had considered, yet, as always, Alkazar had an answer.

"There are many among us who possess gifts, and I remain without a doubt that the eldest of the generations are educated and talented enough to tutor the Tsinians coming of age. I am convinced there will not be cause for the employment of our powers. Nevertheless, should there be an occasion when there is a requirement for their tutor, dispatch word, and I will return without delay. Tis the will of the Changlins."

The council mumbled between themselves. Thya said, "Who can perceive? Perhaps the future will convey with it an addition to the generation of Kapil."

Thya smiled and took hold of Alkazar's hand.

"Very well," Omad declared. "By the grace of the

Changlins, you receive consent to proceed to Earth. I pray your existences be rich and bountiful."

Thya curtsied, and Alkazar bowed. They were about to leave the Escos when Valcan entered the room with Siren following close behind, though she hid in the shadows.

"'Tis a closed session, Valcan, as well you are acquainted with," Omad called. "You are not summoned for."

Valcan stepped forward and bowed. "I beg the council's pardon and yours, my lady. I lay hold to an announcement that will not tarry. 'Tis imperative I discourse upon you as it concerns yourself and Alkazar."

Alkazar escorted Thya to the throne and stood beside her. It was a sight Valcan did not want to see.

"You are granted consent to converse. State your business, Valcan," Thya called.

Siren, who stood slightly behind Valcan, regarded Thya with contempt. She loathed Thya sitting smugly upon the throne with her lover beside her. Inwardly, she was content that Thya's bliss was about to crumble.

Alkazar wondered why Siren was present. He sensed the gathering would not bring joy and stared intently at her, hoping to read her thoughts.

"Siren is with child," announced Valcan. "And Alkazar is the birth father,"

Thya stood abruptly. "She lies!"

"How I desire for it to be a false statement," Valcan answered. "Nay, my lady. Siren is deep with child."

Thya slumped onto her seat; the council were just as stunned. Alkazar fought to control his legs from buckling.

Oh, how Siren wanted to smile. However, she was supposed to be the innocent party and would continue to play her part.

Omad finally found his voice. "Tis indeed a grave set of unfortunate circumstances, and I am regretful for both. Even so, Alkazar, you are aware of your obligation."

Thya and Alkazar contemplated one another for some time.

Alkazar was full of pity and shame. Thya was shocked and tried to understand the turn of events. Finally, Alkazar broke his gaze and stepped down. He walked to Siren and held his arm out to her, which she took, seemingly timidly. Thya watched yet did not believe what she was seeing. Alkazar turned around to face her, his expression full of sorrow and loss. "Tis my duty, my lady," he mumbled. He took Siren's arm and escorted her from the Escos. Valcan followed quietly behind.

The council was silent. Thya sat stunned, unable to comprehend what had occurred.

"A union will be arranged without delay," Omad spoke gingerly. "My lady, you are obligated to attend the ceremony. The wedlock is to be blessed by the Changlins, which results in your consent."

Omad wasn't going to wait for an answer. He deemed it wise to leave and so motioned the council to depart. Omad lingered a moment, unsure whether or not to approach Thya. "I sympathise with your plight. My contemplation and love proceed with you."

He left her sitting alone and there she remained, distraught and ill with woe. It wasn't until Valcan entered the Escos that she stopped crying and wiped her tears.

"My lady," he gently called. "Omad had concerns for your wellbeing and bade me to attend you."

He approached the throne where Thya still sat and took her hand. Thya looked up at him, her eyes red and sore from weeping.

"Relay to him that I appreciate his concern," she answered hoarsely. "I am well and desire to be permitted solitude."

"Nay, Thya, you are far from satisfactory. You are ill with grief," he argued. "A fever is upon you. Unless you come freely, I will be forced to summon an attendant. I realise you do not desire to be a burden to anyone. What do you select?"

"I will depart with you, for it seems the only means to receive peace. Foremost, I desire to visit upon the Changlins."

"Tis fitting," Valcan answered. "And you will, once you partake of this medicament."

Thya took the small bottle Valcan held out and drank the bitter liquid. The solution burnt her throat as she swallowed it, yet it warmed her being, giving her a revival of strength. Soon, she was able to step down from the throne. He wrapped a dark hooded cloak around her shoulders and ushered her from the Escos.

Thya was surprised to see a tril moon. What length had she spent grieving her loss? It felt like only moments ago when her world collapsed. By now, the entire city would have learnt of the occurrence. She wondered if they pitied her.

The Changlins did not lighten her mood, even when they told her that she and Alkazar were destined to be together and not to lose hope.

Valcan wouldn't allow Thya to return to the Recas until he was certain she was well. Instead, he took her to the Tora, under his care. She felt too broken to argue and allowed herself to be ushered away.

Alkazar took Siren to her dwelling where the whole generation of Humals waited for their arrival. He passed Siren's hand into the hand of the head of the family, as was the custom.

"I will receive Siren as my companion and father our child." He spoke with dignity, though inside, he felt like a broken, defeated Bora.

"'Tis how it ought to be. Praise the Changlins," the family chorused.

After the toast, Alkazar left.

Oh, how cruel breath is. He yearned to be with his sweet Thya, yet fate had shown an alternative formula. Their destiny was written, and his and Thya's paths, although mapped, were fated not to cross. If only he could console her, for he deemed her to be as broken as he felt. "Oh, how cruel is fate," he called out unhappily.

Thya and Alkazar's paths did not cross again until the morn of the matrimony. The bride and groom were called to the Escos, where Thya, against her will, blessed the marriage.

"Tis that our love was doomed from the beginning," Thya said. "Despite this, you will forever be in my heart. You receive blessing by the guardian of the Changlins, and I desire health and happiness to your union and that of your child."

How those words cut her sharper than any knife. In front of her stood her love, Alkazar, proud Alkazar. Whether he accepted the justness of it, he did as his duty demanded, stubborn and noble. He would form into a first-class spouse. Though, sadly, he would not be hers. She accepted this, despite the Changlins declaring otherwise. How could she relate to the Tsinians that the Changlins did not bless the wedlock? She was the only one who communicated with the sacred stones, and it would seem done out of bitterness. If any hope remained, she prayed the Changlins voiced it now, for her thoughts were silent.

Alkazar wept silently. Thya had to bestow her

consent to the union. He detested to sight her unhappy yet was compelled by the code to accept his duty. It was his responsibility to raise the child as a Kapil. He would cast aside his feelings for Thya and concentrate on his new family. It mattered not how hard it might be. He wished for his real love's existence to overflow with all the love and happiness she deserved, yet he could not provide it.

Thya was the first to withdraw from the Escos. The council followed, and then the bride and groom were next. The marriage was performed in the Plecky with only Thya, Nimas, and Omad as witnesses. The ceremony was quickly over, and there was nothing remotely loving or romantic about it. Siren swore to love Alkazar beyond others and be a righteous mother; Alkazar promised to be a faithful husband. Once the oaths were over, they left the Plecky amid congratulations and cheers from the villagers. There was concern for Thya's wellbeing, only she was putting on such an act of cheerfulness they assumed she had accepted the situation.

It pained Thya beyond belief to go through the charade, but she knew it would not have looked right if she left before the festivities began. Alkazar kept his distance from Thya and, knowing his wife watched him, tried not to make eye contact.

Three tedious tril moons had yet to pass before Thya's departure. She doubted she could tolerate being around Alkazar for that long. Even though she had barely laid eyes upon him, knowing he was so near was unbearable.

"My lady."

Thya was woken from her thoughts. Athron stood beside her, smiling. "My lady, tis satisfactory for you to withdraw, and I deem you have desired to do so for some duration."

His smile warmed her heart. "Would you be gracious enough to escort my return to the Recas?" Thya asked him.

"It would emit great pleasure, my lady."

Thya made her excuses to Alkazar and Siren then left with Athron.

They walked silently for a while, and at last, Athron said, "Do not renounce hope, Thya, for you and Alkazar are destined to be together."

His speech stopped Thya. "Why do you remark such, good Athron? Tis not the first occasion I have been informed of this. Alas, they are one. Declare to me how you are acquainted with this."

"Am I not the writer of Oracles?"

Thya gasped. "An Oracle has predicted Alkazar and my happiness together. How can this be? Are you assured of this?" Athron pulled an unhappy face at her statement. "Certainly, you are. I doubt you not. What did you sight?"

"You are familiar with the code, Thya. Tis forbidden to disclose an Oracle ahead of the council." Thya looked disheartened. "Despite this," he continued, "what I relate to you has to be maintained between ourselves."

Thya nodded.

"I sight grave moments for both you and Alkazar – torment and pain. Retain your strength, for there is light some distance away. Only when you arrive at this light will you truly be together. For tis written so it will be," he told her proudly.

When they reached the Recas, Thya took hold of Athron's hands.

"I am grateful, Athron, for your assurance. You have permitted me peace. The grace of the Changlins sight favourably upon you."

Athron bent down, kissed her hand, then waited until his princess was inside before leaving.

Although both the Oracles and the Changlins had foretold it, Thya was resolved to forget Alkazar and Tsinia. What good was there hoping for something that could never be. She looked forward to her life back on Earth, now even more so. She missed McDonald's, rock music, and how she yearned to hear infants screaming and children's laughter. She longed for her cosy house and missed her fast-paced job.

Since the defeat of the Senxs, Tsinia had relaxed, and Thya felt idle, as though she wasn't needed anymore. Though there had been many days on Earth when she had wished for lazy days.

Thya spent the following days in the Recas and would not venture outside in case she came across

Alkazar or Siren. She had many visitors calling on her, most bearing gifts for her to take home.

It was the day before her planned departure that Thya decided to visit Siren, believing it was better to leave on good terms. Then, if she had to make an unexpected return, there would not be any bad feelings. It took a lot of courage, only Thya was a proud and determined Tsinian and her mind was made up.

Alkazar's Sacrifice

Thya found Siren alone in Alkazar's dwelling. She preferred to talk to her in private, though it wouldn't have mattered if Alkazar had been present. Thya had not laid eyes on him for some time and needed to prove to herself that she could control her emotions in his presence.

There were no doors to the entrance of the house, and only a muslin curtain stopped the telents from entering the homes. Thya noticed Siren lying on a couch, resting comfortably in the corner of the room. She seemed engrossed in a book and did not see Thya standing outside.

Feeling it was rude to walk straight in and being unaware of Tsinian protocol, she tapped on the side of the porch door. "Can I enter?" Thya asked.

"Your authority allows you this right without permit," Siren answered back.

"Do not rise," Thya instructed as she walked in.

"I had not intended to."

It was going to be harder to converse with Siren than Thya thought, but even so, she intended to attempt her best.

"I realise we will never become allies. Regardless, I desire for Alkazar's sake, whom we both love, that we can be civil to one another. I intend to depart presently, and I am doubtful I will return. If it occurs that we should encounter one another again, I would prefer to feel welcomed by all my subjects."

Thya seated. Siren stared scornfully at Thya. "I have been studying Alkazar's books to gain comprehension of why you are so dissimilar and yet preferable to me," Siren said. "'Tis inquisitiveness that enticed Alkazar to you, naught else. I am satisfied you retain understanding of his interests in diverse cultures and worlds. Once he had sighted your planet, he would soon tire of it – and you." Thya remained silent. "Your world intrigues me," Siren continued. "Do you feel the loss of your homeland? Do you yearn to sight your nation?"

"Very much."

"Then we retain an additional shared sentiment, aside from Alkazar," Siren said. "I agree, as with you, that you do not hold a place in Tsinia. It would be preferable if you departed and did not return."

Thya's anger rose. If anyone else had remarked that, she would have been happy. Knowing it was said in spite and that it was Siren who spoke the words, Thya was ready for a fight.

"I am confident Alkazar would have been satisfied and happy in my land. Do you truly believe you could ever satisfy him? You are delusional. You could never generate happiness. You are compelled to accept that Alkazar was pressured into wedlock. Tis not his own will. Alas, such is fate. I will survive my loss with the awareness that Alkazar will never love you."

Siren rose from the couch and walked to a table laden with fruit. She smiled smugly as she popped a berry into her mouth. She watched Thya thoughtfully as she ate, trying to decide whether or not to reveal her secret. Vengeance, rather than sense, won over, and she laughed. "Tis naught to do with fate."

Siren's statement puzzled Thya, only it suddenly dawned on her. "Your gift of Illusor. I wonder how effective it is." Thya questioned.

It took a moment for Siren to realise what she was getting at. She laughed mockingly. "Nay, Thya. Valcan would not be deceived. Nonetheless, tis clever to imagine such an event. I would not have envisioned such a concept."

"I am aware of this. Tis the difference between us and what entices Alkazar to me."

Thya did not like the way Siren was looking down

at her and so rose to regain eye contact. "I am certain you retain a strong desire to reveal all."

Siren deliberated for a moment. Revealing the truth would not do harm. Alkazar belonged to her now. Even the code could not dissolve the union. In addition, it would present Siren with great satisfaction to sight Thya's expression.

"The baby is not an illusion. I am with child, only Alkazar is not the father."

Thya felt her body go rigid. A familiar fire burned through her blood.

She remembered no more. When she awoke, she found herself on the ground in the forest some distance from the Recas. However, she could not remember how she got to be there. She remembered conversing with Siren, but after which, her mind was blank. Feeling dizzy and weak from fatigue, she made her way back to the Recas. She had hardly stepped through the door when Pertius came running to her.

"My lady, I hold a grave announcement," he gasped. "Siren is deceased, and Alkazar has been seized."

"What?" Thya cried. "Remark that to me again."

"Alkazar is accused of removing Siren's breath. He is bound and requests your counsel."

Thya staggered back. Pertius took her arm to steady her.

"How can this come to pass? I met with Siren, and she was well. Nay, there is an error."

"If that was so," Pertius said sorrowfully. "Alkazar has admitted blame for the fatality and surrendered himself. Nonetheless, he will not divulge what occurred until he converses with you. Will you follow?"

"With certainty, at once. Where is Alkazar being held?"

"He has been bound and escorted to the Escos. We do not possess facilities for incarceration. Tis the first intentional fatality within our great nation."

"We do not recognise that the death of Siren was deliberate. Declare to me, Pertius, if Alkazar is found responsible for Siren's demise, what is the punishment?"

Thya knew the answer, even before he replied.

"Regretfully, the punishment is forfeit of breath. Alas, a trial will not be held as Alkazar has admitted to causing Siren's demise. By the code, Alkazar is accountable."

"I will investigate this."

As Thya entered the Escos, she was stopped by the sight of Alkazar bound to the sidewall of the chamber.

"Release him at once," she commanded.

"My lady, tis not prudent. Alkazar is a dangerous felon," Zarc declared.

"Nonsense," Thya retorted. "You all recognise Alkazar to be a gentle, trusted Tsinian, and until I state otherwise, he will be treated as such."

"What if he absconds?" Zarc dared to continue.

"Alkazar, do you voice your oath that you will not attempt to flee?" Thya asked.

"I surrendered myself freely to the council. I hold not the intention to flee. You receive my oath."

"Very well. Release his bonds," Thya ordered.

Pertius cut the ropes that held Alkazar then left the Escos. Alkazar rubbed his wrists, keeping his face turned away from Thya. He would not look at her, and she noticed this.

"Leave us," she demanded.

"This, I will not undertake," Omad answered. "Whether Alkazar is recognised as a faithful subject or not does not suffice at present. He may have the sickness upon him and is not to be trusted. Tis well advised for you not to be isolated with him."

"I am of a different opinion," Thya objected. "What reason is there for Alkazar to harm me? I will remark again, leave me."

Omad was not convinced. "Yet was there reason for his harm against his spouse and child? Nay, my lady. I will not permit this and will accept any punishment you deem fit."

At first, Thya was angry at his refusal, but then she calmed and felt grateful for his concern over her safety.

"My lady," Alkazar called. "If tis permitted, I would gladly be bound for the sake of your protection."

Thya smiled, thankful for his intervention.

"Omad?" She looked to him for a reply.

"This will satisfy. Be aware I will be yonder if you require my assistance."

Omad departed, motioning to the council to follow. Alkazar's hands were bound behind his back.

"Not too tight," Thya instructed.

Once Alkazar was secure and standing before her, the last of the guards departed. Thya and Alkazar faced one another.

"Oh, Alkazar," she cried. "Do not concern yourself with this folly. Tis my duty to liberate you of these charges."

"Thya, I do not surrender myself lightly. I am guilty of what has passed."

Thya's stomach dropped. "Relate to me what occurred and why Siren lies deceased."

"Upon my return to my dwelling, I perceived raised voices and was startled to recognise one of them belonged to you. I hid and was attentive to what was conversed. I stayed hidden until you had withdrawn then proceeded to enter and confront Siren. She confessed all to me – her lies, her deception. Siren is the cause of our misery. She ruined our future out of spiteful jealousy. I put my hands around her throat and choked her. My mind was cloudy and full of hatred at her trickery. Despite this, I understood my intent. Her betrayal and rebellion against the crown warranted her demise."

There was no hatred showing in his eyes, just pain and misery.

"Nay, Alkazar, there is error in your judgement. Siren did not deserve this. And what of the innocent child? I cannot and will not believe this of you. You do not retain one drop of immoral blood in your body. You would not deliberately remove breath."

She caressed his cheek, and he turned his face inwards, nuzzling into her hand. She embraced him and they kissed, his fevered tongue tasting, lapping like a hungry animal.

Not a moment had passed since marrying Siren when he did not long to hold Thya in his arms. Although he tried to ignore his feelings, his desire for her never left.

"Grant me absolution, Thya. To perceive it from you will bestow strength to cope and contend with my impending doom. Oh, how hopeless this is."

"Do not surrender hope, my love," she pleaded. "I will converse with Pertius. There has to be some means to reverse the judgement. I will not permit this."

"My darling Thya. Sweet princess, how I love you."

They kissed until she stepped away. "I have been presented with a belief that all will be well. Both the Oracles and the Changlins remark that we are destined to be together, my love."

"Oh, if this was genuine," he cried. "Even so, I deserve my punishment. I removed Siren's breath and that of an unborn. I recognise my crime and accept my punishment."

"Do not remark such. Oh, Alkazar, why has fate played such a cruel hand? Do not abandon hope. I will return with glad tidings. This I am confident of. Rest easy, aware that you possess my love always and forever."

She kissed him softly on the lips, and after brushing away her tears, she made for the door.

Alkazar watched her leave. "Thya, how I love you," he whispered. "I desire you never discover how I sacrificed for my love of you." He watched Thya stagger towards the exit.

Again, the power had weakened her strength. His dying desire was that she acquire the skill to control the strange force inside her.

After the door to the Escos closed, Alkazar fell to the floor, once again a broken man.

Thya walked out of the Escos with as much dignity as possible. Many had gathered around the building, waiting to hear more on the scandal.

"Zarc," Thya called, "you are entrusted with the task of attending to Alkazar. Untie his binds and bring him refreshments and fresh garments. Treat him as you would a loyal Tsinian. If I perceive otherwise, you will be dealt with by me. Is this understood?"

"Your command will be obeyed, my lady."

"Valcan, tend to Alkazar's wounds. Sight that he is comfortable and that his mind is relaxed."

"It will be done."

"Pertius, I require your counsel. Omad, prepare in readiness for Siren's ceremony," she instructed.

"Will you not disclose what you ascertained," Omad asked.

"Not at this instant. Alkazar is not in the correct mind to be judged. Please be patient." She left with Pertius trailing behind her.

"Advise me, Pertius. Is there naught I can do to prevent Alkazar's death?"

"I am currently searching just this. I yearn to locate a means to stay the punishment. Alas, so far, I am unsuccessful in my findings. I am optimistic that I could find a clause in the ancient code. Tis necessary for me to hold an understanding on what was conversed if I am to aid him."

"Alkazar has informed me that he removed Siren's breath, although I will not disclose why."

"Tis grave. It does not fare well. I will exert myself in aid to Alkazar."

"I require another reply prior to your departure," Thya said. "Would the queen of Tsinia retain the authority to permit leniency?"

"I am satisfied the queen of Tsinia would possess influence. Nonetheless, I am unfamiliar with how much power you would have. I will attempt to discover this at once." Pertius gazed thoughtfully at

Thya before asking. "If you are considering what I imagine, then indeed your love for Alkazar is strong. Tis a huge sacrifice, Thya. Deliberate carefully prior to deciding. I believe that love as strong as yours and Alkazar's cannot be prevented even by demise. Rest well, my lady."

Thya smiled and turned to walk into the Recas.

"I hold an opinion, my lady, if I am permitted to express it."

She turned and bowed her head in acceptance.

"I do not consider Alkazar capable of committing such an evil act. He has not the heart."

"I am in agreement, good Pertius." Thya smiled. "Locate me if you retain disclosure. It matters not the lateness."

She turned and entered the Recas. As soon as the door closed, she collapsed.

Thya woke to find the stern and worried faces of Valcan and Omad staring down at her.

"What has come to pass?" she whispered.

"I fear the strain has taken its toll on you, my lady," Omad explained. "Your suffering is great, and Valcan will agree that you will not be fit to depart for some while."

Valcan was silent.

"I do not intend to depart as yet, so concern yourself not."

Omad appeared content with her answer. "With

your permission, my lady, I will withdraw for there is much to prepare."

Thya dismissed Omad with a wave of her hand, which then fell limp to the bed. Valcan walked Omad to the door, closed the door after him, and ran to Thya's aid.

"Valcan, what has occurred? I sense your distress."

"You are on the brink of fatality, princess. I revived a little of your strength so not to alert Omad on the seriousness of the situation. There is not a natural remedy that will heal you. The only prevention will be the employment of my power. You will slumber, and when you are wakeful, you will be healed and feel refreshed."

"Why be so cruel?" Thya whispered. "If you love your princess, permit her to slumber evermore and do not awaken her to this nightmare." Thya then mouthed the words, 'Only when you arrive at this light will you truly be together.'

Valcan couldn't make out her words and did not ask for she had fallen into a deep sleep.

When Thya woke to find Valcan asleep by the side of her bed, she felt revived and strong as though she had slept for days. She nudged Valcan gently, waking him from his doze.

"Oh my," he exclaimed. "Pardon, my lady. The employment of our gifts generates exhaustion, does it not?" He gazed at her questionably before continuing, "Are you refreshed?"

"I am, as you declared I would be. How did you come to discover my fatigue?"

"After tending to Alkazar's hurts, he bade me attend you in the belief you would require assistance. I praise the Changlins that he did."

Thya remembered Alkazar's plight and sat up in alarm. "Oh, my poor Alkazar," she cried. "Has Pertius called upon me? For what duration have I slumbered? Is Alkazar with breath?"

"Worry not, Thya. Your endurance of slumber failed for your attendance of Siren's farewell. Pertius, too, was not sighted. Tis believed he is scrutinising the ancient code and has been for some while. Alkazar is active, and I am certain you will desire to know he is being treated justly."

Thya tried to smile, but it was too difficult.

"My lady, twice I have met with your unique fatigue, though this is the severest I have witnessed. You barely survived. I am in requirement to understand what causes this ailment. I believe a successive attack could possibly be your last. I conclude that a will or power not of your own drains you of strength, energy, and even your essence. Reveal to me, did you employ your gift of late?"

"Not of my awareness," she answered, but a realisation hit. Oh, Alkazar, she silently cried.

Being in a sudden need of Alkazar's counsel, she plotted her escape. Turning to Valcan, she said, "Only one Tsinian can respond to your query.

Unfortunately, he cannot be summoned forth. Hold onto your belief and notify me of any new conclusions. Meanwhile, I present you with my oath: I will not employ my power until it can be deduced why this occurs. You demand me to rest, and I will if you withdraw."

"With certainty, my lady. I will depart promptly and begin my study of this difficulty. Already, it has lost me rest. Never has an ailment defeated me, and I am determined to understand it. By your leave." He bowed.

As soon as Valcan left, Thya jumped out of bed and got dressed. She climbed over the balcony and made her way to the Escos.

She found Alkazar asleep on the soft pillows that had been laid on the floor. Thya ran over to him and fell to her knees. "Alkazar," she whispered. "Alkazar." She nudged him slightly, stirring him from his sleep. "Alkazar, wake up."

This time, he woke with a start. "Thya, why do you appear?" He sat up in alarm. "You ought to be resting!"

"So, you recognised the symptoms?"

"Symptoms? What symptoms do you speak of?" He looked at her. "I summoned Valcan to attend to you in the cause of your distress. I was aware of how ill you were becoming. Are you rested?"

"I am compelled to convey something to you."

He tried to interrupt, only she put her fingers to his lips.

"Permit me to continue," she said. "It did not occur to me until Valcan quizzed me on my gift. I am getting ahead of myself, am I not?" She took a deep breath then explained what she could remember of the happenings in Senx.

Alkazar listened intently. He was disturbed and angry to learn of Kovon's attempt to subdue her. He had concluded for himself most of what had occurred.

Thya shook her head. "I do not recall the attack upon Kovon, yet I am convinced I put those horrific afflictions upon him. None were present, and he was not capable of harming himself to such a degree. I understand that it was I that caused him to suffer so terribly."

"'Tis what he deserved," Alkazar commented.

"Yet, I recall naught. I sight destruction. The sight sickened me and will remain in my memory for as long as I breathe. I understood at once that it was my doing, and I believe the same has occurred since." Alkazar shifted uncomfortably. "I recall conversing with Siren in your dwelling, though I do not remember departing as you state I did. Then, I discover myself some distance away from your abode with no awareness of how I came to be there."

She watched Alkazar's expression hoping to get

some answers. But he stayed stoic as he remembered all too well that sorrowful morn.

He was about to enter his home when he heard raised voices, so he hid around the corner. Listening to the argument, he was shocked to hear Siren confess he was not the father of her child. Anger exploded inside his body, only he suppressed it when he heard someone gasping, as though short of breath. He ran to find Siren holding her throat; a seemingly invisible hand was crushing her windpipe. He faced Thya and was amazed to see a bright light emitting from her eyes.

She was past the Owto. His only hope had been to deliver her from it.

"Thya," he called. "You recognise this voice and hold trust in it. Be attentive to what I remark. This voice calms you. Follow it, Thya. Return to me."

Thya turned to face him. As she did, Siren fell to the floor.

"Thya, heed the sound of the voice and follow it."

It was obvious to him that something else had control of her. This was not her own will at work.

"Thya, if you can perceive me, I require you to pursue my voice. I am located in the centre of a yellow field. I am standing in wait for you. Pursue my voice. Can you perceive me?"

"I heed you," a ghostly voice rang out.

"Approach the direction of my voice. I am waiting. Walk through the field. The wind is blowing. The scent of grass relaxes you. You are close. Pursue my voice. Soon, you will encounter a dark, hollow space. Do not side-step this. I require you to halt in front of the hollow space. Do you comprehend?"

"I do," she replied.

Already, her voice was softening, and her eyes seemed to dim. He had some control over her at least. Though he deemed it dangerous to continue, what other choice did he have?

"I am present," she told him.

It was too late to stop. He had to continue and pray he could bring her back.

"Thya, step into the black, hollow space," he commanded. Thya's foot moved as if unsure what to do.

"Concentrate, Thya. Regard only the sound of my voice. Do as I command. Proceed onwards."

As soon as Thya's foot stepped into the black hole only she could see, she fell into Alkazar's waiting arms, unconscious. He laid her gently on the floor then lifted one of her eyelids. Her pupils were back to their normal colour. He had done it. He had brought her back. Praise the Changlins. But could her powerful connection to the Changlins be the cause of this possession?

He left Thya and went to Siren's aid, only she was beyond help, even from Valcan's gift.

He felt compelled to transport Thya away with haste prior to her awakening. She need never discover what had occurred. It was not of her doing, yet he doubted the council would understand. The penalty for removing Siren's breath would be to forfeit her own. Thya's existence was worth more than any other Bora, including his own.

Alkazar came back to the deadly serious present.

"And then there is the fatigue," Thya continued. "A side effect that drains my strength and energy. You sighted upon this yourself. Valcan declared I was close to fatality when he discovered me. You were aware of this, were you not? That is the real reason you summoned him to attend. You sensed my ills."

Anxious hearing of the seriousness of her wellness, he praised the Changlins. If anything were to happen to her now, it would all have been for naught.

"I will declare what I believe occurred."

Alkazar remained silent.

"I terminated Siren — rather, the power within me did. You either sighted the attack or arrived to discover Siren's body. It either means what you are undertaking is wrong. If I am the blame for Siren's demise, which I am convinced I am, then I alone ought to suffer, not you. Alkazar, my love, your existence merits two of mine. I will not permit you to sacrifice yourself for me. I will surrender myself to the council, explain what occurred, and hope they will be lenient. I hold no doubt Valcan will agree with my findings. Already, he retains suspicions."

Alkazar's heart raced. He never guessed Thya would realise her involvement, and he had Valcan to contend with also. Surely, if Valcan knew of the situation, he would defend her, rather than sign his princess's death warrant. It was a risk Alkazar was not willing to take.

"Nay, Thya. I did not retain comprehension of your unique power, and it grieves me to be informed of your plight in Senx. I am grateful for your frankness, for I believe carrying the burden of your dark secret has eaten away at you for some duration. I understand how you arrived at your conclusion, and if I could, I would aid you in gaining an understanding of this second power you deem to possess. Only, I assure you, my love, tis not you who removed Siren's breath. I watched your departure. At that moment, Siren was breathing. I even observed you walking through the forest. I can only conclude that in the shock of Siren's confession your mind blanked. I believe Valcan will concur."

Alkazar hoped he had convinced her. Thya stared into his eyes.

"Then why did you eliminate Siren? Why did you not converse with the council? I believe there is a clause that could have annulled your wedlock."

Alkazar sighed. "My anger possessed me. I had not control. I despised her for the grief she brought upon us. I had not thought for the child, and I am saddened by its death, though not for Siren's."

"It pains me to perceive you utter those words," Thya cried.

It cut Alkazar to speak them. He was certain Thya would not converse with Valcan, and the dark secret would lay undiscovered. This only left his farewell to Thya.

"Light will shortly be upon us, my love. The sands are running low. My breath will be removed come the next tril moon. Despite this, you, my love, will continue with yours. I implore you to depart prior to my demise."

"I cannot. I will not!"

"I will not permit you to witness my conclusion. You have suffered enough distress," he argued.

"You behave like a Tsinian who has lost all hope. Pertius is studying the ancient code. He believes he will discover a clause —"

"Thya, there is not a means. Death is the punishment for death."

"Then I will accept the crown," Thya announced. "I will become queen and pardon —"

"Nay, Thya, I would not permit you to sacrifice your freedom for me. Your authority, though great, would not extend far enough."

Thya fell to her knees. He stroked her face. "Do

not weep, my love. We will encounter one another again, and then we will be together for eternity. We are one, Thya. Never disregard this."

"This is what he meant. Athron stated that we would unite at the meeting of a bright light. Only then would we truly be together. I understand now. Nay," she cried. "I will not permit this. It cannot come to pass. I will not lose you."

Alkazar took Thya in his arms and embraced her. "While in my solitude, I reflected upon my past. It appears as some strange illusion as though naught occurred. Having you present in my arms is as genuine as it gets, and the memory of your smell and touch will forever be in my heart. Remain with me, Thya. Permit me to touch you once more."

They made love for the last time – beautiful, slow, sexual love. Every moment, every kiss meant and held.

As they lay beside one another, Thya struggled to stay awake, but eventually, her eyes closed, not knowing if it would be the last time she would see him.

Alkazar would not waste precious moments in sleep. For the rest of his short life, he wanted to look upon his love. He intended to sacrifice his existence to spare hers. Though the conclusion was close, he was not unhappy. He was grateful. He was sick of this cursed existence. Why had it all gone so wrong when everything was once perfect? How he desired for it all to be a crazy dream he could wake from.

"Rest well, my darling Thya, for you will not lay sight upon me again."

The light did not bring joy with it. Alkazar was still awake, watching Thya sleep, when Valcan entered the Escos.

"I imagined I would locate our lady here," he whispered.

"She is near to waking. I implore you, dear Valcan, lay upon her a deep slumber until her departure. She has been through so much. I cannot bear to surmise her pain and anguish."

Valcan agreed. He raised his hand over Thya's eyes and held it there for a moment. "Tis done."

"Summon Omad to my council," Alkazar instructed.

He kissed her lips before he picked her up and placed her into Valcan's arms. He wanted to scream at the unjustness of it, only he could not make a sound.

He was gazing out of a small window when Omad arrived. "Will you permit a condemned Bora a final desire?"

"Certainly," Omad replied.

"When our lady awakes from the false slumber, which by my request Valcan has put her under, I ask that you announce to her that the judgement was brought forward by my order and I am deceased. When she implores you to reveal my body, which I deem she will, inform her the body was burnt and my ashes scattered. You will announce to all my desire. Our lady is not to lay sight on me again. This is my ultimate request."

"It will be carried out, Alkazar." Omad looked to the floor. "If it were in my power, if I held any influence, I would not permit this to pass. You believe this, do you not?"

"With certainty, my loyal friend. We exist by the code, and we expire by the code. Now, please, permit me my solitude. I desire not for visitors."

"Very well," Omad said and bowed mournfully.

"My lady, tis the duration for your departure. You ought to hasten to the orb."

Thya opened her eyes. Once again, she found herself lying on her bed. Omad, Pertius, and Valcan were present in the chamber.

"It was dark when last I shut my eyes." She sat up in alarm. "Where is my love? What has occurred?"

Pertius sat on the edge of the bed and took her hand. "My lady, it saddens me to be the one to bear you grave tidings. As his final desire, Alkazar requested that his judgement be brought forth."

"This cannot be!"

"By the law of the code, Alkazar's breath was removed."

"Surely you jest." She smiled. "He would not have requested this of you." She turned to address Omad. "Declare to me Alkazar is fit and well."

Omad did not dare utter the lie. He lowered his eyes to the floor.

"Why did you grant him this?" she cried. "Why?"

"He did not suffer pain," Omad informed her, hoping his words would make a difference.

"I begged him not to abandon hope, Omad. The Oracles prophesied our destiny together."

Omad looked to Valcan then to Pertius, for they had not been informed of the Oracle of late. They had no answer for her.

"We ought to hasten if you are to depart, my lady," Omad reminded her.

"Certainly, we will," she replied. "Only, first, I desire to bid farewell to Alkazar. Where is he laid? Where rests his body?"

"Alas, under his request, his body was burnt and his ashes scattered," Valcan told her.

"Then tis over," she spoke without feeling. "I remain with naught, not even a chance to pay my respects. There is naught to prolong my stay. Send me away from this cursed land. I am prepared for departure."

She walked through the city as if in a dream, wondering if she would remember her duration as an illusion, a figment of her imagination, or recalled as genuine memories.

The citizens of Tsinia came to bid her farewell. All were tearful by her departure and the sorrowful story the name Thya brought with it. Would she be remembered as their saviour, the princess who defeated the warlord of Senx, or would it be the memory of her fatal love for Alkazar that burned into their memory?

Her faithful servants bowed their heads as she expressed her gratitude.

"Valcan, you have surpassed your loyalty to me. I could never repay you for your aid. I will miss you, dear friend."

Valcan bowed and kissed her outstretched hand. A tear dripped down his cheek. He was too choked up to reply.

"Pertius, you instructed me well, and yet there is much more I could absorb from you."

"I appreciate your kind expression, my lady. Yet I am doubtful there is more I could tutor. You grasped an understanding so bizarre I cannot fathom. You were familiar with the code prior to our beginning."

"I desire upon you a contented existence, and I demand you wed soon." She smiled at her own words.

"Good Athron, you bestowed hope to me when all was lost, and for this, I will always be grateful."

Athron took hold of her hand and squeezed it gently.

"Heed the Oracle, my lady," he told her. "Though

all seems lost, tis far from over. Do not fail to retain faith."

Thya smiled at him. If only she held as much belief as he. She would indeed retain a contented existence.

"Dear Omad, our parting bears with it great sorrow, though, regretfully, I will convey to you I hope we never encounter one another again. I feel I possess naught, save sad memories. Regardless of this, I present my oath and will retain it. If Tsinia is ever in requirement of their princess, I will return. I entrust the ruling of Tsinia to you. Sight that my land is rich and rule my subjects wisely. Bestow your vow to me that you will not hesitate in my recall should the need arise."

Omad took hold of Thya's hand and bent down on one knee.

"I pledge that if Tsinia is ever in requirement of its princess, you will be summoned without delay. Remain with you the light of Tsinia."

Omad placed a chain around her neck. On it hung an oblong-shaped, grey crystal.

"If one of your own steps upon Earth, you will receive awareness. The crystal will light in warning of their arrival."

The orb then began to appear.

"To my kinsmen," she called out, "Thya, princess of Tsinia, guardian of the Changlins, desires for your lengthy existence and contentment. We could encounter one another again. If this does not come to pass, never forget your plight and how fortunate you are. Farewell, my friends."

Thya did not know of another Tsinian, some way off, who was speaking his goodbyes.

"Farewell, my love. 'Til we unite again. My love will stay in your heart evermore," Alkazar whispered out of the window of his temporary prison.

Just before Thya stepped into the light, she became alert, as though she had woken from a strange dream. Questions raced through her mind.

Where would she arrive? How long had she been absent? Did she still have a job? She looked like someone who had emerged from a fancy-dress party. It was too late to worry about that now. She would soon come face to face with those dilemmas.

Squeezing her eyes shut, she stepped into the circle of bright light.

Thya's story continues in

The Quest

When Haty notices a Tsinian crystal glowing, she knows she must stick to her word and return to her homeland as Thya. Knowing her kinsmen needed her, there was no hesitation. Even though there was more to lose than just her life.

Once more a prophecy informs the reader of oracles that only Thya could stop the war and save not just her people, but the rest of Enumac from Kovon's psychotic plans.

Along with three other companions, Thya is sent on a perilous quest to locate a crystal eye which holds an evil known as the Dark Force.

The group is tried and tested throughout their journey by monsters, death and courage.

New friendships will be formed and others lost.

Acknowledgements

Thank you for buying and reading Illusional Reality. This has been an ongoing extremely enjoyable project for a few years now and to see the novel published is such a thrill. I hope you had fun reading it.

My thanks to everyone who has helped me through this journey and for bringing my vision to life.

Huge thanks to my amazing editor Michelle Dunbar and to Julie Hoff Stafford for her continued love and support.

From the Author

Karina is a freelance writer, a prolific author of thirteen books, narrator, VA and promotional designer. As well as hosting a radio show and being YouTuber. Oh, and when she's not helping other authors, she's listening to rock songs, watching reality shows and just loving life.

Come and say hi, I love chatting with my fans:
Author.to/KarinaKantas
On Twitter: twitter.com/KarinaKantas
Blog: urbanhype101.wordpress.com
On Facebook:
www.facebook.com/ExplosiveWriter
Illusional Reality Duology: bit.ly/IRFBPAGE

Sign up to Karina's mailing list and you'll receive a free gift.
eepurl.com/daKie